HER FORBIDDEN FANTASY

WOMEN OF PARK MANOR

ANGELA SEALS

ROSE GOLD PRESS, LLC

Editor:
Nicole Falls
Cover Design:
Sherelle Green

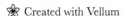 Created with Vellum

I want to thank the ladies whom I had the pleasure to work with on this awesome series: Sherelle Green, Anita Davis, Elle Wright and Sheryl Lister. Thank you, ladies, for this awesome journey! I will be forever grateful!

ACKNOWLEDGMENTS

I would like to thank my family and lit sisters for their continued support in my writing journey. A warm thanks to my readers for giving me the confidence to continue to do what I do. I hope you enjoy the Women of Park Manor!

Happy Reading!!!

PROLOGUE

SKYLAR

"$\mathcal{I}$ didn't even know Buddy's old ass, so why in the hell am I here?" Slurring those crude words made me down another shot of tequila, as I leaned against the circular bar located in the back of the tavern. Maybe I'd had too much to drink. But who was counting? The half bottle of tequila I'd finished off in my apartment, before coming down to the tavern, gave me a good indication that I should call it quits.

Swirling the ice cubes in my glass, I observed the Park Manor residents who had come out for the door-man's memorial service. Park Manor Tavern was packed with everyone in the complex in attendance. I had just moved into the upscale community a week ago, and I had no clue who any of these people were. I glanced to my left and noticed an elderly gentleman placing his dentures on the black linen-covered table to eat. *Ugh!* I thought. *What happened to having table manners?*

Focusing my attention back onto my diluted drink, I figured I should thank my next-door neighbor, Mary. She had practically dragged me down the steps to the attached tavern to pay tribute to a man I only remembered seeing at least five to six times. Her annoying voice still rang loud in my ears. *"Come on, Skylar Johnson! Be a good neighbor and show some respect."* I had told that broad several times to just call me Sky, but she insisted on calling me by my government name. Now Mary's nosey ass was nowhere to be found in this place of AARP members.

Chuckling to myself, I caught sight of a sparkling designer cane, heading in my direction. The aged woman sent a wink my way as she hobbled across the floor to her seat. *I bet one of these women was Buddy's old ass lady.* I giggled, while signaling the sexy ass bartender over for a refill. For one quick moment, I tried to remember if this was drink number seven or eight. Shiiit, I didn't know. All I did know, was ever since I'd stepped into this tavern, I'd been overwhelmed with grief.

The bartender sent a nod my way, alerting me to give him a second while he served a few other patrons. I tilted my head toward the ceiling in annoyance and inhaled slowly, trying to release the sudden lump that had formed in the center of my throat.

A tear threatened to fall, as my eyes watered with unwanted emotions.

"I see Buddy's passing is really affecting you."

Sniffling, I focused my gaze on the blackest pair of eyes I had ever seen. The bartender's eyes reminded me of Edward Cullen from the *Twilight* movies. Taking in a deep breath, I tried to focus on his lips. Big mistake! Those chocolate dumplings looked very kissable.

I shook my head to get rid of the lustful thoughts that ran through my mind. Because, truthfully, all I wanted to do was choke out a sob.

"Yeah, you can say that," I lied, knowing my tears weren't for Buddy, but the less people knew about me the better.

He nodded and retrieved a clear bottle from the top shelf. After filling the glass halfway with tequila, he topped it with a splash of a small amount of orange juice in the glass.

"Actually, I wanted that straight."

He lifted an eyebrow. "Wow! I thought maybe you should take this one with a chaser." Smiling, he revealed a dimple in his left cheek.

Screw you, sexy beast! is what I wanted to say. Instead, I snatched the glass from his grip and took a long swallow before the lump returned. Apparently, it was no use, because a traitorous tear slipped down the side of my face.

Placing his masculine hand over mine, he said coolly, "Buddy meant a lot to some people around here." He paused when a man whistled our way. He nodded in his direction and continued, "He was a cool dude. The ladies seemed to like him." He chuckled. "Well, the women in his age group."

I smiled, enjoying the feel of his rugged hand on mine. He must've caught on to the fact that he was still touching me, because he jumped back and slid those thick hands in his pockets. *He could probably touch my soul*

3

with those long fingers. Mercy! Shit, a one-night stand didn't sound bad at all.

"It's these damn drinks," I mumbled to myself, peering down at the glass in my trembling hands.

"Did you say something, beautiful?" the sexy bartender asked.

Yeah, I said I'd like to pour this tequila on that dark chocolate skin of yours and lick every drop. Instead of telling him that tonight I wanted to be a freak, I just waved him off. "I didn't say anything."

"Hmmm. Are you from around here?" He folded his arms across his wide, muscular chest.

I cocked an eyebrow.

Raising his hands in defense, he tried to explain, "No, I think I hear a country, southern twang in your accent."

My southern roots seemed to follow me everywhere I went. No matter how much of a conscious effort I made to not let the southern twang come out, I always found myself defending it.

"I'm from Alabama," I admitted, smiling sheepishly. Downing the last drop in my glass and hissing at the smooth burn, I absentmindedly turned the glass sideways to make sure I got every drop. I didn't believe in wasting good liquor.

"A country girl," he stated, his tone one of surprise.

Nodding, I focused my gaze on the folks moving back and forth in conversation. It was either that or continue to stare at the huge, bulging print in the middle of his jeans.

I had been going on a good year without the touch of a real man. I felt the itch creeping up in my midsection with each crooked smile he gave me. By the way the bartender just ran his long tongue across his straight, white teeth, I had an unnerving feeling that he was reading every lustful thought in my head.

Fidgeting with the empty glass on the bar, I tried to figure out if I was going to ask him to join me for a night session in my apartment upstairs. Until I heard the man from earlier whistle again across the bar. He threw his hands in the air in frustration and mouthed something offensive our way.

"Excuse me, miss," the bartender said in annoyance.

I watched as he trudged away. The tip of loneliness began to set in again. I was fresh out of drink. And I wasn't sure how much confidence I had in my walking ability right now. So, I stayed put. Leaning across the bar and watching everyone filled with emotions. Tears and sobs filling the room with every passing second.

I needed to get out of here. Putting myself through this torture of attending another funeral was something I wasn't ready for. I closed my eyes and still could picture my father's white casket sitting at the front of our small church. His passing was fresh—it had only been two weeks since I had to say goodbye. It was the hardest thing I'd done in my life. Well, not exactly. Sitting outside of the house that belonged to the killer who'd shot my father with a loaded twelve-gauge shotgun probably topped the list.

The asshole was on trial for a double homicide and my father was the sheriff of the town we lived in—Buck, Alabama. He had been the arresting officer and one of the prisoner's escorts to court. The man had struggled, getting loose from one of the police officers, and pulled a gun from my father's holster. He shot him in the chest, and afterwards, stood over his body with a smile.

5

The prisoner's family was involved in the cartel and had enough money and connections to post bail. I wanted to kill him, contemplated on how I would do it. He had taken everything from me. The only thing that saved me from a dark road was the gold chain I wore around my neck with my mother's picture. It willed me back to my good senses.

The next day I received a call from the FBI telling me that my application to become an agent had been accepted. Wanting to follow in my father's footsteps, I packed my bags and headed to Santa Monica, fleeing from the pain. But it seemed no matter how far I ran, I couldn't escape it.

A tap on my shoulder, snapped me from my daydreaming.

"They want us to all take our seats."

I gazed up at the woman displaying a gold tooth and faded red lipstick. I needed badly to get off my sore, aching feet, so I nodded. Spotting a seat in the corner, I tried to make my way over, until my right ankle wobbled in the three-inch black pumps I was wearing. That little mishap, let me know that the half a bottle of tequila I drank in my apartment before coming down, had joined in with the drinks I'd now consumed at the memorial service.

A headache began to pulse at my temples. Flopping down in a nearby chair, I placed my head in my hands to try and massage away the pain. It was no use, because I had done it again, drank myself into a hot mess. Pain wasn't something I could deal with. Hell, no one should have to bury two parents in their lifetime.

"Excuse me, miss."

"Awww, c'mon," I huffed, frowning at the familiar voice.

"This is someone's seat," the same annoying lady from earlier stated. "You have to find your assigned seat."

Who in the hell assigns seats at a memorial service? Not giving it too much thought, I stood, and wobbled, staggering my way back to the bar. My pumps flopped from the heel of my feet. Geesh, I had to find a seat fast as the tears filled my eyes again. I just couldn't take it any longer. I had to get out of this place.

Spotting a familiar face waving me over, I forced my left ankle to walk straight. I swatted away a few tears and squinted to get a better view. It was Teegan from my floor.

Yes!

When I staggered over, Teegan stood and greeted me. "Your seat is over here. Skylar, right?"

I slid my body into the brass chair. "It's just Skyyy," I slurred.

My teasing headache had now turned into a marching band. The vibration radiating from my head caused me to place my forehead down on the tabletop.

"Sky," someone called out.

Feeling a blast of air, I raised my head. I could have sworn my face had fallen off when I didn't feel my lips any longer.

"You can't do that here, hun. Are you okay?" the standing woman asked, sounding genuinely concerned.

Focusing my gaze on the woman flopping down in her chair next to me, I said, "I'm fine, I just haven't gotten much sleep." I let out a long, forced yawn to prove my point.

The salt and pepper haired man on the mic cleared his throat, causing everyone to direct their attention to the front of the room. Leaning back in my chair, I glared at the four women sitting at the table. Of course, I knew Teegan. Last we talked, she had revealed to me that she was into massages and self-healing. I wasn't sure what she did, but it all sounded like voodoo to me. To my left sat Paityn and Kathi—two tenants I vaguely remembered meeting at a mandatory fire drill the other day. I learned Paityn sold sex toys and Kathi was a pharmacist. Glancing to my right, I couldn't recall the lady's name, but remembered it was the same as a color. She was the same woman who just nudged me awake from my brief nap, and Park Manor's Leasing Manager.

Closing my eyes briefly, I glanced back over to the lady sitting next to me and wondered why she was staring at me so curiously. *Blue! That's her name.* I frowned. *Naw, that's Beyoncé's daughter. Ah ha! Burgundy, that's it.* I forced a smile and directed my attention back to the front of the room.

With every passing moment, it seemed like a different person got up and talked about Buddy. I wasn't sure if he was a nice man, mean man, or an annoying man. But one thing I could tell, he had his way with the women. My head did a deep dive toward the tabletop, but luckily my reflexes kicked in. I glanced around the table to see if anyone was looking. Thankfully, the women were engrossed in small chatter.

I fidgeted with my fingers to try and gather my composure and find the leg muscles to get the hell out of this tavern. But then I had an eerie feeling come over me. As if someone was watching me. I was sure it was the drinks playing tricks on my consciousness. Jerking

8

my neck to the left and then to the right, I nearly screamed out loud. Burgundy was burning a hole in the side of my face.

"Is there a problem?" I asked her.

"Would you like me to assist you to your apartment?"

Everything in me wanted to take her up on her offer. However, I was in control of myself. I didn't need help. And for her to think so, must've meant I was out here not holding my shit together.

"No, I'm good."

Standing, Burgundy gripped my arm. "I know what you are. I can help you. Please, let me help you," she insisted, with a stern gaze.

I shrugged her hand from my bicep. She was starting to piss me off. What the hell did she mean by she knows what I am? Was that some type of Morse code I was supposed to decipher?

I leaned down to whisper in her ear, "Burgundy, I think you're probably a nice person. But I'm leaving and I need you to back off."

We locked eyes for a moment. I thought I saw pain and hurt lurking in her pupils. But I didn't have time to figure out what her angle was. I just needed her to move out my way. "Burgundy, I really need you to move around," I said, while side stepping her to find the exit door.

Obviously, she didn't get the hint that I didn't want to be bothered because she was right on my heels, guiding me by the tip of my elbow toward the door. My first thought was to jerk away. But then my ankles started doing that weird twisting thing and I realized I needed her for support.

Reluctantly I accepted her help toward the elevators as I stumbled a few times and Burgundy caught my fall.

"We're almost there, Sky," she murmured, placing an arm around my waist.

It was a good thing she was walking me to my apartment, because the breakfast I ate this morning seemed to be making its way up my constricted throat. I didn't really want to mess up this pretty leopard print dress I was wearing with vomit. So, I leaned my head against her shoulders.

To my surprise, she didn't shy away. Instead, she escorted me like she was familiar with the process. She looked too calm at this moment, and it worried me to have to put all this trust in someone I barely knew. *I wonder what she thinks of me?* was the floating question in my head. However, as we stepped onto my floor and I wobbled down the hall, I couldn't help but to be real with myself.

I didn't want to admit it or accept the fact that I had become something I had long despised. I became even more nauseated as I barely unlocked my door to my apartment and jetted to the bathroom. As I puked up the contents of my stomach, the question haunted me, *how I was going to hide the fact that the FBI had just hired an alcoholic?*

CHAPTER 1

*S*ix Months Later ...

KAREEM

"I don't give a flying ass if you can't do twenty push-ups. That sounds like a personal problem, Adams," I huffed, pacing the football field. *It's too early in the morning for this shit*, I thought.

The new recruit held back unshed tears as she sniffled once and stood before me in formation—arms at her sides and head titled upward, staring me straight in the eyes. I admired how she held her own, not faltering or allowing my curt words to send her running in the opposite direction.

"Sir, I can't do anymore push-ups, I caught a cramp," she whined.

Squaring my shoulders, I stepped forward to close in the few feet between us. "If you can't give me twenty, you're done, recruit," I ground out between clenched teeth.

I guess I had spoken to soon, because Adams' ass burst out into a stream of never-ending tears. I stared at her, giving her time to catch her breath and wipe away the waterworks. Little did she know, this was a test. If she couldn't take my scowling words, then she wasn't cut out for this line of work. The skills to be an FBI agent came with discipline, tough skin, and the ability to stand your ground.

In my eight years as Senior Special FBI Agent Kareem Hawks, I'd seen many recruits come through my boot camp that didn't last the first week. My job was to weed out the weak, the wannabes, and the ones that didn't belong.

I used to feel remorse for the newbies I cut in the first two days. However, now I just didn't give a damn.

"Adams, find your way off my field," I huffed. "Tears are for babies and not for FBI agents."

She sniffled a few times, trying to wipe away the tears. "P-Pleaseee," she stammered. "Give me another chance. I can't go back home and explain to my parents that I failed yet again at another task. I didn't finish college, sir, and this was my last attempt to make my dad proud," she cried.

Inhaling slowly, I pointed to the agency building. "You're done, Adams. Move it."

She covered her red face and ran toward the building with loud sobs. I swallowed hard, focusing my attention on the rest of the fifty recruits staring at me. Fear was evident in their eyes. I didn't care. I wanted them to receive the message that I was a hard ass. In order to become an agent, they had to come through me. And what they didn't know, was my graduation rate was low ... like really low.

Pacing up and down the rows, I didn't utter a single word. Yet, I did it more for intimidation. Rounding the last row, I caught sight of one of the recruits whispering something to another recruit.

"No one speaks on my watch," I yelled. "I own y'all asses for the next thirty minutes, and I don't remember asking anyone for their damn opinion." I stopped short in front of a recruit whose nametag had Johnson printed on the front.

"Is there something you want to say, Johnson?" I screamed in her face.

"No, sir," she bellowed, standing with her legs gapped apart and her hands behind her back.

I'd had my eye on Johnson for a few months now. I was impressed by her drive and her ability to push past the fatigue and pain. And I couldn't deny her natural beauty. Her hair was pulled back in a bun, and she had a few brown freckles speckled on her nose. I had a fetish for women with thick curves. It should have been a sin the way her white T-shirt stretched across her ample breasts, revealing how well-endowed she was in that area. Although, I'd love to see how one of those chocolate buds tasted in my mouth, I told her, "Drop and give me ten."

"Yes, sir." She dropped down and counted out, "One, sir. Two, sir. Three, sir."

She continued all the way to ten. Afterwards, she hopped up and went back into formation, staring me straight in the eyes with a sly smirk.

I'll be damned! I thought. To say I was impressed would be an understatement. Let's just say Johnson had my attention. I stood there staring at how her boobs were jingling from her heaving chest. However, I wanted to wipe that smirk from her cinnamon-colored face.

"Give me ten jumping jacks," I barked.

She stretched her hands above her head and started out with the same count as before. Only this time, when she got to ten, she did an extra jumping jack, taking her count to eleven.

"We have a smart ass," I said, pacing the grassy area in front of the squad. I've had recruits like her before. Trying to push the limits. Sending a message that they could take any punishment I tossed their way. I was about to make her wish she'd never stepped a foot on my field. Forming my mouth to give her ass another exercise, my counterpart, Agent Starks, who was standing at the front of the line, clapped his hands and dismissed class.

I frowned, turning around to give him a piece of my mind. How dare he dismiss my goddamn class? He had no right. Plus, I ranked higher than him.

I heard a giggle as the rest of the recruits fell out of line and started making their way across the field. Turning to face Johnson, I screamed. "I'm not done with you yet. I haven't dismissed your ass."

She went back in formation, placing her arms around her back. "Yes, sir."

Licking my lips, I pointed my index finger in her face. "You speak only when spoken to," I warned.

"Yes, sir," she bellowed again.

With those final words, I clapped my hands twice to dismiss her. She turned and ran off to join the other recruits. I couldn't help but to watch Johnson jog away. The woman was built like a brick house and that ass …

it should be banned for being so perfectly round. *Damn, I don't know what's wrong with me.* I ran a hand down the side of my stubbled jawline. I'd seen many asses and boobs come across my class. *So why am I so infatuated with this one?*

"Agent Hawks!" Anthony Starks called out to my fleeing back. I slowed my steps to allow him to catch up to me.

"Same ole Kareem busting asses," he chuckled. "Did you really have to fire Adams?"

"Man, she was a weak link, I had to cut her," I said with no hesitation. "Why you acting like you so brand new to my tactics?"

Starks shrugged his shoulders. "I was hoping one of these days, you would change." He narrowed his eyes. "You were about to go *in* on Johnson's ass."

I chuckled. "How did you know?"

Starks smacked his lips. "I saw how she was taunting you with every exercise drill you threw her way."

"Yeah, I saw that shit, too. She'd better be glad you came to her rescue. I was about to have her ass running sprints across this field." Starks laughed. "Which brings me to my next point." I stopped walking to face him. "Don't you ever dismiss my class when I'm handing out drills."

Dropping his shoulders, Starks sighed. "Man, I'm just trying to save you from yourself. I feel like sometimes you take this job too far."

I bellowed, "There's no such thing as going too far. I'm doing my damn job." I placed a hand on Starks' shoulder. "I'd advise for you to do the same and get your heart off your damn sleeve."

A few droplets of rain begin to fall as we started to sprint to the building. "Whateva, man. At least I have a heart," Starks huffed. "You may need to find yours." He glanced my way with a frown. "Did you know that some folks at the agency have given you a nickname?"

"A nickname." I smiled, marveling at that revelation. I had vaguely heard a few rumors around the bureau from some agents saying that I was known as a heartless monster. "Naw," I lied. "What are they saying?" I questioned, acting unfazed.

Approaching the building, Starks opened the steel door, allowing me to enter first. "Man, they are calling you Godzilla."

"Ha," I laughed, leaning against the beige walls. "And do you agree?"

He turned toward me with a smirk and said, "You're my bruh, Kareem, we go way back. But you have to lighten up."

I raised an eyebrow.

He lifted his arm to explain. "I love you like a brother, but I've watched you over the years. You're turning into your father, man. I miss the fun, joking Kareem. Now everything is sooo serious."

Sucking my teeth, I glanced down at the army fatigue boots I was wearing. It should've been an insult to hear Ant voice those words. But these days I'd become numb to criticism. "I'll keep that in mind," I said as I entered my office and slammed the door.

Walking over to my window, I folded my arms across my chest and gazed out at a line of recruits doing laps around the field. It was a gloomy November day and a few weeks away from Thanksgiving. Perhaps Starks was right. Maybe I did come off a little too strong. We went way back to my old neighborhood in Boston. He had become my best friend; we were two bad ass, knuckle-headed boys, always getting in trouble and playing pranks on our parents.

I scratched my head, remembering the time I had told Ant to play like he was dead. Since he was a skinny boy it was easy for my burly arms to pick him up and take him to his mother. I busted through the flimsy, black screen door, with Ant's loose-limbed body hanging from arms. I told Mrs. Starks that Anthony was hit by a car. The loud squeal that radiated from her petite body made Ant jump from my arms.

That day was the last day of our outlandish pranks. Ant swears his mother beat his ass for seven days straight. And once my father got wind of my antics, I couldn't sit on my butt for a month.

However, when we went to college our pranks continued again. We pledged the same fraternity and after we both became Kappas, it was our turn to hand out chores and tasks to the new pledges. We would egg rooms; pour flour, hot sauce, and pickle relish on all the newbies' clothes. We would chase the freshmen to their classes with a thick, wooden paddle. If they were caught, it was an automatic five swats across the ass.

Damn, we were bad.

We were both accepted into the bureau at the same time, which made us grow up and take life seriously for the first time in our lives. It was a lifelong dream of mine to be a part of something that had meaning. I'd always loved *Criminal Minds*, *Rookie Blue*, or anything that resulted in catching the bad guys.

In my thirty-seven years I'd never married. My career had become my obsession. It was all I lived for. It was the only thing that I was good at. Being this way was the only reason I graduated top of my class. Earned the top spot as the best agent in the bureau. And I guess became known as Godzilla and a heartless monster.

I chuckled.

You would think to be known as a monster would be hard for some folks to swallow. The difference between me and other folks was that I didn't give a fuck. My father was ex-military. He drilled life lessons in me and my sister. She was now overseas in Korea as a sergeant for the Army. I was sure she was making some poor kids' lives miserable.

I could still hear my father's words echo in my ears. *"If you want life to take you serious, you have to grab it by the horns. Make it pay attention. Give it your best shot. And remember being second is not good enough."* I carried that motto with me throughout life and in everything I did. That was one of the reasons I would not accept less than perfect from my recruits.

Which brought me to Skylar Johnson. She was the best recruit I had on the field. But I couldn't let that be known. I couldn't show favoritism and praise her for all the challenges she overcame. I had to treat her like all the other recruits. And not the woman I'd dreamed about over the past month. Adjusting my pants, I took a seat on the edge of my desk. Damn, I was getting horny just thinking about her now.

On the field, I had to always catch myself from stargazing. No one could ever know about my infatuation for her. I would become the laughingstock of the bureau. I could hear the rumors now. *Godzilla likes one of his students!* Damn, I couldn't let them see.

A knock at the door snapped me from my reverie.

Rounding my desk, I took a seat in my maroon chair. "Yeah," I yelled.

The door cracked open, and the face that appeared from the other side made me let out a fake cough to drown out the sudden gasp that had echoed through the room.

CHAPTER 2

SKYLAR

*K*icking myself for even considering coming in here after he caught me talking on his line was on the top of my mind. I paced in front of his office for several seconds with Bella on my heels. She was another recruit who I had become friends with over the past months. She'd warned me not to come in, practically begged me on hands and knees. I told Bella I thought it wasn't fair how he cut Adams. Granted, she couldn't keep up and do the exercises, but she was trying. However, that wasn't why I was standing in his office doorway now.

Dammit, why did he have to look so good today? He was wearing a white v-neck t-shirt, army fatigue pants, and boots. And that sexy ass trimmed goatee, connecting with his sideburns, sent a rush of heat toward my clitoris. I was a sucker for a well-groomed man.

"Excuse me, Agent Hawks, can I enter?" I asked.

Leaning against the door jamb, I waited for him to close his mouth from the gasp I heard escape his parted lips. He shuffled a few papers on his desk and waved me in. Taking three steps forward, I wondered, *why he had to be so damn sexy?* I wanted to hate his ass, call him ugly, wished he would fall off the face of the earth. But the sad part was all I wanted to do right now was run and jump into his big arms. The man had a body like The Rock from WWE. I wanted to taste those luscious lips and circle his Adam's apple with the tip of my tongue. I wondered how good he would taste with a bowl of vanilla ice cream drizzled over him.

"At ease, recruit," he said.

Placing my arms behind my back, I closed my eyes briefly. I envisioned myself climbing up this six-foot beanstalk and nibbling on a hard, muscular honey-golden body. However, that wasn't going to happen because I had to remember, *he hates you.*

Clearing my throat, I focused my attention on the setting sun outside of the window to refrain from looking into his strong, handsome face. I had no clue what I was going to say. I was hoping the two shots of gin I had just taken in the locker room would soon kick in and ease my nerves.

"How can I help you, Johnson?" he inquired, bringing me back to the present.

"Ummm …" I began, but nothing else came out as my eyes darted quickly around his minuscule office, soaking in the few plaques and gold medals hanging from the walls. It seemed like a football trophy was in his windowsill. I glanced at his glass desk, in search of a wedding picture. I couldn't fathom anyone wanting to marry a man like him. But I heard some women were into the asshole, controlling types.

I tried to speak again when I noticed him frowning down at his sleeping laptop. Clapping my hands together, I said, "Sooo, we can skip the formalities and you can just call me Sky." Then I laughed!

Silence enveloped the room as I cringed in my skin. My big ass mouth had said something wrong. But why was he staring at a dark computer screen? For the first time since I entered his office, he lifted his head and locked eyes with mine. Leaning back in his chair, he crossed his legs. "Is that right?"

I nodded. "Yes, sir."

He sat forward. "Let's get something straight, maggot. I'm your superior officer, not your friend or homie. I would never address you by your first name. You're Johnson."

Did this fool just call me a maggot? I decided to not let his cruel words faze me. I expected this type of behavior from him. Men like Agent Hawks didn't really scare me easily. What he didn't know was I came from a family of law enforcers and he only ignited the fire in my smart-ass mouth.

"Sir, with all due respect," I began, "yes, I know I'm Johnson. That's the name I was born with. Second, there's nothing you can say to rattle me." I narrowed my eyes to bring emphasis to those words. "I came in here to ask you if you wanted to come to the restaurant in my building with a few recruits and officers. I'm hosting a Friendsgiving celebration." I paused. "I just didn't feel right leaving you out."

Smirking, he stared at me with no response. I started to think maybe I had gone too far, and I was going to be recruit number thirteen being kicked out. Until he opened his mouth. "Nothing I say can rattle you, huh?" The way he said it, it was more of a statement than a question.

I nodded, waiting on the next insult to be thrown my way. Instead, he stood from his chair, which caused me to take a step back.

The lines on his face softened. "I'm intrigued, Johnson."

Not sure if I should take that as a compliment, I remained quiet.

"I'll have to decline your offer," he stated coolly. "I don't fraternize with my recruits. However, it took balls for you to come in here today."

I smiled, knowing he had a heart in that muscular chest of his.

"If that's all, you're dismissed, Johnson."

Turning, I opened the door.

"Hey, Johnson."

I glanced over my shoulder, which was a mistake, because the burning gaze he gave me made me wet my panties. I swallowed hard as my mouth became dry. And just when I thought he may be feeling the same way as I did, I heard …

"Although you had balls to come in here today, I still don't think you have what it takes to become an agent."

Asshole! is what I wanted to say. Instead, I replied, "We'll see about that, sir," and closed the door behind me.

&

I hurried into my bathroom to grab my favorite

23

maroon lipstick in the medicine cabinet. After painting a light coat over my lips, I smeared the lipstick over to the edges of my mouth with the tip of my finger. Twisting back and forth in front of my floor-length mirror behind the bathroom door, I wondered if I had gone too far with the four-inch red pumps I had on. I had paired them with black fishnet tights, black mini skirt, and a red, fitted, spaghetti strap tank top.

Feeling like a schoolteacher, I snatched the clip from the ponytail I had formed on the top of my head, allowing my reddish natural curls to fall in my face and gather around my neckline. *This is stupid!* I shook my head, while staring in the mirror. I had only invited a few Park Manor residents and agents from the bureau for a Friendsgiving celebration. I had wanted to do something special in memory of my father. However, I was the only one who knew the real reason around me wanting to join together the only people I knew in Santa Monica.

I strutted back into the living room, fixing myself a drink from my mini bar. I gazed out of the floor-to-ceiling windows, admiring the ocean views in the near distance. Thanksgiving was my father's favorite holiday. He said it was a time to reflect on things we were grateful for. Besides being in Santa Monica, working on becoming an FBI agent, and snagging the last un-renovated loft in the upscale community, there wasn't much more I was thankful for. This complex was too expensive for me to afford on an FBI recruit salary but accepting one of the lower-end lofts suited me just fine.

Admiring a few parasailers in the distance, my mind drifted to Agent Hawks. It was a risky move to ask him to come out to my little party. But I was drawn to him like a magnet. Stupid should've been my middle name. Because all the man ever did was insult me and tell me how I didn't belong. But deep down, I still felt like there was a kind soul underneath. *I wonder if he'll reconsider and still come to the party? Do I want him to come? What would I do if he did?* All of these questions were driving me crazy.

I let out a heavy sigh. A knock on the door had me rushing over to my kitchen sink and pouring out the remnants of my drink. Grabbing a peppermint off the countertop, I popped it in my mouth. I opened the door to a smiling Bella.

"Hey, Sky," she sing-songed, pulling me to her for a hug.

I peeled Bella's hand from around my neck. "Hey, Bella." I grimaced. She could be a little too much sometimes with her hugs and kisses. She was Swedish but raised as an Army brat. She was immersed in so many different cultures but stayed true to her Swedish upbringing of showing affection. I had explained to her that Americans were not into all the kisses and hugs.

"I think this is a wonderful thing you're doing, Sky." She trudged over to the window. "I mean, getting everyone together was a challenge, but your infectious smile won them over." She squeezed my cheeks.

I swatted her hands away. "C'mon, Bella, we have to get down to the restaurant to greet everyone."

Bella bounced toward the door, as I grabbed a few bags from my couch and countertop to finish setting up. I locked the door behind us as Bella continued to chat all the way to the first floor.

"Sky, are you listening to me? I told your crazy ass not to go in Agent Hawks' office today," Bella screamed over the singer, Tank, whining through the loudspeaker when we entered the restaurant. A few agents and residents had already arrived.

I rolled my eyes, placing a turkey centerpiece on the table. "Bella, stop being dramatic. I just extended the offer I gave everyone else."

"Uh huh!" she said, taking a shot of vodka. "He's not like everyone else, Sky. The sooner you realize that the better off you'll be." She stepped closer to me. "I was told to stay out of his way, and I might graduate."

I waved her off. "I'm not in his way," I assured her, moving over to the buffet table to make sure the sandwiches were stacked neatly on the serving tray.

Bella was right on my heels. "Sky, you be saying shit to piss him off, and those smirks you give him are only gonna make it harder on you."

Giggling, I turned toward Bella. "Maybe I want to piss him off."

Bella raised both of her hands in the air. "Geesh, I guess I'll come and visit you in the unemployment line."

I tuned her out and started humming the lyrics to one of Chris Brown's songs, "Wall to Wall". Strutting over to the bar in the corner of the room, I ordered a Sprite. As I placed the last centerpiece on the round table, I sipped on my drink, while glancing around at the agents from the bureau dancing and enjoying themselves.

I realized all of this wouldn't have been possible without Burgundy's help. She was the leasing manager for Park Manor and was able to work out an affordable rental price with the building management team. I was glad we were able to connect again.

I thanked her for the day she helped me to my loft. She had told me if I ever wanted to talk, her door was always open, and she added that she was great listener. I assured her that I was on the straight and narrow, although I saw doubt lurking in her eyes.

As I moved my hips to the music, I was glad I had lost Bella in the shuffle of partygoers. However, it didn't stop me from thinking about what she had said. Maybe I was pressing my luck with Agent Hawks. But the man turned me on in the worst way. Most people ran from his spitfire, but my dumb ass welcomed it.

Shaking my head, I pulled a silver flask from my purse and spiked my Sprite with a splash of gin. I had started drinking at the age of sixteen, after finding my mother dead in her sleep. Over the years, my drinking increased from only drinking socially to drinking every day to every couple of hours. Now, at the age of thirty, I think I had become what people called a functioning alcoholic. My father never knew. Or maybe he did. Perhaps that's why he'd sent me to countless therapists. Whom I found something wrong with all of them—a reason to never return.

Kathi, Teegan, Burgundy, and Paityn caught my line of sight as they floated over to the DJ booth. Within minutes the "Cupid Shuffle" blasted across the loudspeakers and a few women ran onto the floor. I shimmied my way over to where the ladies stood. I had gotten to know everybody well from a sex toy party that Paityn had thrown a few months back.

Rubbing shoulders with Burgundy, I said, "Thanks for coming out, ladies."

Paityn slapped me on the shoulders. "Girl, you're welcome. But that music was dry as hell until we just told the DJ to switch it up."

Kathi snorted and said, "I actually liked the song that was playing before."

Burgundy grunted, bringing her drink from her lips. "Who in the heck wants to hear 'The Thrill is Gone' by BB King?" She laughed. "That shit was like back in the seventies."

Kathi lifted her hand. "Ummm, it was actually the eighties."

Everyone tumbled over in laughter. Kathi was the buttoned-up type, more conservative. She always wore neutral colors and once said that she wished she could wear bright colors but realized only certain types of women looked good in them. I thought maybe that was her way on throwing shade on me because every time she saw me, I had on an eye-popping, bright piece of clothing.

Gathering my composure, I turned toward Teegan. She always had this Lisa Bonet vibe going on, with her long draping dresses and hair tied in an African decorative headscarf. "Gal, do you have any openings at your massage parlor?"

Teegan rolled her eyes heavenward. "It is not a massage parlor," she corrected me. "I give people natural ways to heal their minds, bodies, and souls."

Smacking my lips, I replied, "Okay, whateva. When do you have time to do that to me?"

Burgundy chuckled, and Teegan blew out a heavy sigh.

"I'll call you," Teegan replied, sounding exasperated.

She was annoyed with me, and I knew it. Sometimes Teegan and I didn't see eye to eye. But at the end of the day we respected each other.

Paityn steered the conversation into her hosting another sex toy party.

Kathi interjected, "How did you get into selling sex toys again?"

That was a question I wanted to know as well. But my eyes were drawn toward the front door of the restaurant. A few agents pooled around the entrance, laughing and conversing with someone I couldn't get a good view on yet. I moved closer, ignoring the thought in my head telling me I didn't want to know.

"Where are you going?" I think I heard Burgundy ask in the distance.

Without answering her question, I stopped short of the last table separating me from the visitor. When the last agent stepped back, my breath momentarily hitched.

I couldn't believe it. Agent Hawks had come to my party. I should've been ecstatic. Over the moon. But the slender arm draped across his made the hairs on my arms stand up.

His eyes locked with mine, but I couldn't stop my stomach from twisting in knots because of the beautiful woman gripping his bicep. She held a hand to her mouth and laughed at something Agent Starks, who was standing to her left, said.

Envy twisted my stomach even more as I admired her long, black, straight hair—comparing it to my curly, tangled locks—her hazel eyes, and petite frame. On the other hand, I had brown eyes and curvy hips. Licking my parched lips, I tried to run in the opposite direction. Until Bella caught the swing of my arm. "Why do you look like you just saw a ghost?" she asked.

Shrugging my shoulders, I turned toward Bella, needing a distraction. "Talk to me," I said anxiously.

She looked like a deer caught in headlights, when she frowned and replied, "I am talking to you."

I nervously gnawed on my bottom lip as I caught sight of Agent Hawks and the woman making their way toward me. Letting out a boastful laugh, I slapped her shoulder. "You're so funny, Bella."

"Johnson!" Agent Hawks bellowed from across the room.

I turned as my stomach did a nosedive toward my feet. Mustering up the best smile I had, I said, "Agent Hawks, glad you could make it."

CHAPTER 3

KAREEM

The deep scowl on Sky's face had me wanting to explain. I didn't know this was the party she was trying to invite me to. Truth was I shouldn't even be here, and especially not with the woman hanging from my arm. I glanced between the two women and they both seemed to be sizing each other up—with the lifted eyebrows, pursed lips, and folded arms. I shook my head, thinking about the chain of events that had transpired to lead me to this moment.

I had just sat in my car for the past thirty minutes, contemplating if I was going to leave or stay. Mercedas had said she'd be down over twenty minutes ago. She knew it was hard to find parking at the Park Manor complex. This place stayed busy with its many shops, restaurants, movie theater, and residents moving to and fro.

Parked in the fire lane, I could see through the glass of the restaurant that there was some sort of party going

31

on, which would explain why there weren't any visitor parking spaces available.

"Move it, asshole!" a man shouted from behind me in a grey Mustang.

I flipped him off and pulled into the only available spot that had just become vacant. Making my way inside of the building, I gave a head nod to the doorman standing in the valet booth. Mercedas' ass really wasn't worth all this hassle I was going through. We had just met three weeks ago, and this was our fourth date. She was a beautiful woman, well-educated, smart, and had a great job. But there was something missing.

What was missing? I wasn't quite sure. Let's just say I didn't get that warm, fuzzy feeling for her. But what I did know was I couldn't get Skylar Johnson off my mind. After she had left my office the other day, I had gone through her file. It was the typical bullshit that most recruits wrote about why they wanted to be an agent. Her records were too stellar, squeaky clean. The only thing that stuck out the most to me was the fact that her father was law enforcement. He was killed in the line of duty.

Also, her file revealed that she scored high on the entrance exam, and that she graduated top of her class in college. I skimmed down to her lie detector test. Certain parts of her responses were inclusive. Now I wondered how she was accepted. I dug a little deeper to review her questions and my access was denied. That was a first. I'd been an agent long enough to know when something didn't smell right. Sky was hiding something, and anyone who came through my class I'd sniff out the bull and expose it for what it was.

Now I was standing in the lobby of the Park Manor complex, and from behind me I heard, "Kareem!"

I turned to see Mercedas stepping off the elevators.

She sashayed over to me and placed a kiss on my cheek. "I'm so sorry to keep you waiting." Stepping back, she gave me a once over. "You look good tonight."

I smiled, giving her an appreciative gaze as well. Mercedas wore a purple, short dress that dipped low in the front, revealing the split in her cleavage.

"You ready to go?" I asked.

She nodded and grabbed ahold of my arm as we made our way toward the revolving doors.

"You decided to come after all," a familiar voice said.

Smiling, I turned around to greet Ant. "Bruh," I threw my hands in the air, "I'm coming to pick up my date. What are you talking about?"

Ant grinned. "Oh, so you didn't know that this is the little spot that Sky is throwing her Friendsgiving party at?"

Shaking my head, I pointed to the restaurant door. "Is that where she's having the party?"

"Yep," he confirmed with a grin.

Shit, I thought. "Aight, Ant, we gonna get out of here before anyone sees me."

My words were short lived because the double doors swung open, and I was greeted by a few agents who recognized me. Before I knew it, I was being escorted into the restaurant.

After giving fist bumps to a few agents, I tried to usher Mercedas' ass out the door by the small of her back. However, she was loving the idea of finally meeting some of my coworkers.

"Oh my gosh, Kareem, I'm so happy I got a chance to meet some of the people you share time with." She giggled.

Nodding, I scanned the room slowly, until I saw her. Sky and I locked eyes. Her deadpan expression turned into a look of surprise. Tugging at Mercedas' arm, I tried to usher her back toward the exit. It was no use, because the closer Sky got, the more I tried to flee. But Mercedas kept resisting me. Holding me in place as she conversed with Ant at her side.

Once she was in proximity, I scratched the back of my head and thought, *damn she looks good tonight.* Her hair wasn't in that messy bun she always wore on the top of head. Tonight, her hair flowed around her shoulders. *And that fuck-me outfit she has on would only be worn in my bedroom. Not in public. Only if she was my woman. Which, she's not.* But that didn't stop how good she looked. *Damn good! Good enough to eat, and lick. Fuccck, Kareem get your head in the right spot. Remember, you've been a dick to her. You even called her a maggot. I'm an idiot. Yep a fucking idiot.*

"I'm glad you could make it," Sky said.

Shaking my head, I brought my mind back to the present. I turned toward Mercedas when she cleared her throat. "This is one of my recruits, Johnson."

Mercedas curled her lips in a frown, and Sky lifted an eyebrow. I intervened in the stare down. "We were leaving."

Smirking, Johnson folded her arms. "Well, I'm glad you were able to come to the party."

"Actually, I live in the building," Mercedas interjected. "We were on our way to see Fantasia at The Coliseum."

I gave Mercedas a side eye. Who asked her to share that information?

"Oh, that's wonderful. I love Fantasia," Sky stated. "I hear she puts on a great show. You two have fun."

"Oh, we will!" Mercedas said with sarcasm oozing from her tone.

I didn't miss the daggers and eyeroll Sky sent her way before she smacked her lips and directed her attention to me. "I'll see you at work."

With those final words, she strutted off and became lost in the crowd.

&

The rest of the evening seemed to move in slow motion. I checked my watch for the sixth time tonight and it was a little bit after midnight. The Fantasia show was awesome, but I couldn't get Sky off my mind. The expression on her face from earlier told me that just maybe there was more between us than either one of us wanted to admit.

Mercedas chatted all through dinner about taking things to the next level and how I was exactly what she was looking for in a man. I wasn't sure how she came to that conclusion, when she didn't even know much about me. Other than I worked for the FBI. Which was probably all she needed to know.

"I had such a wonderful time," Mercedas stated, laying her head on my shoulders.

We cruised down Ocean Avenue in my Ford Ranger. Adjusting my rearview mirror, I said, "Thanks, I had a great time, too."

She glided her hand down my chest, gathering my

blue Giorgio Armani shirt in her hands. "I just can't get enough of you." She inhaled close to my ear. "I've been waiting to give myself to you and I think tonight is the night."

I kept my eyes on the road, with one hand on the steering wheel and the other on the gear shift. There was nothing Mercedas was saying that made me get a hard on. I just didn't get that *forever* feeling with her. I wished I did, but it wasn't there, and I needed to stop lying to myself.

"I don't think that's a good idea, Mercedas," I said, pulling up to the Park Manor complex.

She frowned. "What?"

Turning off the engine, I shifted my body toward the passenger seat. I wasn't good at break-ups. Never really did them face-to-face. A text message or voicemail was more of my thing. Letting out a sigh, I said, "I think the past couple of weeks together were great. We had fun. But I don't think *we*," I pointed between the both of us, "are good together."

Gazing out the windshield, she opened her mouth and then closed it. She ran a hand through her straight hair and blew out a long breath. From the side view of her face, her expression made her look like she'd been just hit by a dumpster truck.

"It's her, isn't it?" She glanced my way.

Not really understanding, my brow furrowed. "What are you talking about?"

Mercedas smacked her lips. "The girl in the restaurant." She pointed at the Park Manor building. "The one you introduced as Johnson."

"Oookay," I said.

"I saw the way you looked at her, Kareem. You've

never looked at me that way. I hoped one day you would. But the more I tried to force us I could tell you were a million miles away." She smiled. "I should be mad but I'm not."

I massaged the back of my neck. "I don't know what you think you saw, Mercedas, but Johnson is my recruit. That's all."

Chuckling, she opened the car door. I rushed around to the passenger side and helped her out. We walked up to the complex, and once we reached the entrance, she turned to face me. "Your recruit, huh? If you can't be real with me, be real with yourself, Kareem." She gazed at me for a moment, placed a kiss on my cheek, and walked inside.

Standing outside of the complex, I placed my hands in my jean pockets and peered through the window of the restaurant. All the lights were turned off and I didn't see anyone moving about inside. I walked back to my car and got inside. Mercedas was way off base. I didn't have a thing for Johnson. *So, why were you hoping to see someone in the restaurant just now? Why do you dream about her? And why every time she's near you, do you get an electrifying feeling?*

Shut up! I tuned out the thoughts floating around my head.

Cranking the engine, I pulled out onto the street. Even if I wanted it to be more between us, there was no way I could cross the lines from being her boss to being her man.

CHAPTER 4

SKYLAR

"*H*old the bag steady," I instructed Bella as we did punching bag drills inside of the FBI combat facility. Wiping a bead of sweat from my forehead, I punched the bag with everything I had in me. The mighty force sent Bella sprawling backwards, hitting the floor with a loud thump.

"Sky," she squealed. "I think I just broke my tailbone."

Running over to where Bella fell, I extended my arm to help her up from the floor. "I'm so sorry, girl. I don't know what came over me."

A few recruits stopped their punching bag drills and glanced our way. We were standing in the middle of the room surrounded by bags, and sweaty men and women during various physical drills.

Bella shook her head. "You've been in a funky mood these past couple of days."

I nodded. "I know I have. I don't know what's wrong with me." I placed my head in the palm of my hands.

Bella stood rubbing the side of her hip through her black capri leggings. "Does it have anything to do with how the party turned out last week?" she moaned.

I blew out a heavy sigh and pushed out, "No," as I trudged over to a side bench.

Bella followed me, limping on her right leg. "I really think I broke something," she whined.

"I'm sorry," I apologized again. I glanced her way, fixing a few strings from the messy bun on top of my head. "Can you keep a secret?"

Bella nodded.

Honestly, I was tired of keeping the secret to myself. I thought I was going to burst in flames if I had to keep walking around like everything was fine. I locked Bella with an intense gaze. "I swear you can't tell nobody."

"I won't," she reassured me. "C'mon, tell me now. You're scaring me."

"Okay," I said. "He's driving me crazy. I think I'm literally losing it. I can't sleep, eat, or think." I slapped my forehead. "He has a girlfriend and he hates me. Why would someone be attracted to someone who hates them?" Before Bella could respond, I continued. "Me. I'm the idiot who thinks about a man who can't stand the sight of her," I huffed.

Bella placed a hand on my heaving shoulders. "First, Sky, breathe. Second," she paused, "who are we talking about?"

My mouth gaped open. "I said all of that and you have no clue who I'm talking about?"

"I'm sorry," Bella cried.

"Agent Hawks, duh. Who else would I be talking about?"

Bella shrugged her shoulders. "I don't know, but definitely not Agent Hawks. Wait," she snapped her fingers, like she had just solved a great mystery, and gasped, "you like Agent Hawks."

I quickly slapped my hands over her mouth as a few people looked our way. "Can you keep that shit on the hush?" I whispered.

Bella mumbled something and I realized I still had my hand over her mouth. "Dang, Sky," she blurted. "You can forget that relationship. It's never going to happen."

"Thanks for the confirmation," I said.

"Not only is he your commanding officer—" Bella's words were cut short, when Agent Hawks and a few higher-ranking agents walked into the room and blew a loud whistle to get everyone's attention.

The hairs on the back of my neck stood up as he pulled a clipboard from under his arm and stepped into the boxing ring positioned on the right side of the facility. "Gather around, everyone," he shouted.

The recruits stopped punching the bags and staggered around the outside of the ring.

"Today we're going to be working on taking down your opponent. You must figure out a way to get your partner off their feet. I'll go first, to show you different techniques." He peeked down at the clipboard. "I've paired everyone in twos. But the only person who's left out …" He paused, scanning the paper in front of him, then glanced up and said, "Johnson! You'll be with me today."

If I could shit bricks right now, I would've probably

shit out a ton. "Did he just say my name?" I whispered to Bella. I knew I heard him wrong. There's no way I could be paired with him.

She slapped my back. "He sure did."

I held my breath as I took what seemed like the longest walk ever to the ring. A few recruits moved to the side to let me pass. I climbed the three steps with ease and bent down to slide between the ropes. Standing on the opposite side of the ring from Agent Hawks, I watched as he glanced my way. He handed over the clipboard to Agent Starks and walked toward me. His black muscle shirt showed off his hard six-pack. And his black, baggy jogging pants gave me a clear view of his length. Swallowing hard, I tried to direct my eyes anywhere else.

He'd taken off his shoes somewhere before entering the ring. I hadn't realized I was still holding my breath until he was standing in my face. Exhaling, I began to sweat as he placed his large hands on my shoulders. *Sweet Jesus! Why would you torture me like this?* I think I instantly became moist.

"I need you to turn around," he stated.

Moving like a robot, I turned around with my back facing him and waited. For what? I wasn't sure. Until, the hard feel of him crushed against my ass and one of his hands wrapped around my waist. *Jesus Christ! If this man doesn't unhand me, I'm going to die from my heart leaping out of my chest.* He wrapped his other hand around my neck and stepped one leg in between my legs.

"This is called a single leg takedown," he yelled.

Before I could blink an eye, my legs came away from under me and I was being lifted in the air by my waist. I came down on the mat with a thud.

Agent Hawks bent down and whispered, "Are you okay?"

I nodded and accepted the hand he gave me to stand upright. I hadn't notice that I was holding on to the hem of his T-shirt, until he grabbed my waist again and spun me around.

"Now, take me down with a double leg takedown," he instructed.

My head was dizzy from how close he was holding me. I could smell his potent aftershave. I lifted my gaze to his stubbled face, and he held a tight scowl. His eyebrows were furrowed, and for the first time I noticed the dimple in his chin.

My knees buckled and he gripped me tighter. "Are you sure you're good?"

Licking my lips, I nodded. He pierced me with his slanted brown eyes. I wanted to reach up and sample those luscious chocolate lips. I had a thing with lips and kissing was my expertise.

"Double leg takedown," he reminded me again.

I spread my legs apart and wrapped my arms around his waist. I could feel the double beats of his heart as I laid my head against his chest. Without warning, I swept both of his legs away from under him. I must've forgotten to let go, because we both went plunging to the mat. Opening my eyes, I discovered my face was buried in his chest. I felt something protruding against my belly button. I started to connect the dots, and realized I was straddling Agent Hawks. That wasn't his hand poking me in the stomach, and the heavy breathing wasn't mine.

"Ummm … I'm so sorry," I said, using his biceps to push myself upward.

Agent Hawks cleared his throat and frowned. "This is how you don't take someone down," he said to the class, pointing my way with disappointment oozing from his tone. "You don't lose balance and fall on your attacker." He stood up, once I found my balance. "I want everyone to get with their partner and practice the different takedown techniques." He moved to the corner of the ring. "I've already demonstrated two ways. Now, I want you to add on the other four. Underhook, Overhook, Bear hug and Duckunder."

He clapped his hands. "Let's get to work."

The other recruits shuffled around to find their partners. I had slipped out of the ring and fled to the women's restroom. Placing my hands on the sink, I gazed into the mirror. My skin was flushed, and my ponytail was in disarray. I released the flimsy rubber band from my thick curls and allowed them to fall in my face.

I was a mess out there, I thought. Out of frustration, I slapped the sink. I knew how to do a double leg takedown. I could do it in my sleep.

But today I had made a fool of myself. And the worst part of it? Agent Hawks and the rest of the class saw straight through me. My mom told me long ago, *"Don't show everyone your cards. Leave them guessing to the very end."*

"Guess what, Mom?" I said to the small mirror. "I showed my cards today. Your daughter is an utter failure," I whined.

A click of the door had me reaching for a paper towel and dabbing my eyes. "I know, Agent Hawks is looking for me," I said to the visitor. "Tell him I'll be out in a moment."

Silence filled the space and I slowly turned around. Gasping, I clutched the sides of the sink, until my knuckles turned white.

"Agent Hawks," I said breathlessly.

He advanced toward me with slow, calculated steps. His hands rested behind his back and his face was unreadable. "I came to see if you're okay."

Pointing to myself, I glanced back and forth around the two-stall bathroom. "Who, me?" I asked.

He chuckled. "Yes, you."

"Oh yeah, I'm fine," I lied.

He stepped forward, closing the small distance between us. My breathing slowed as he reached out to smooth a string of my reddish, curly coils behind my ear. "I'm glad to hear that," he murmured, slightly above a whisper.

Who is this man staring at me with so much care and concern? I asked myself. *Why's he here?* He'd just fired someone for running off and crying. *Is that what he came in here to do to me?*

The thought left my mind as he grazed my cheek with the back of his hand. He lifted my face to meet his eyes by a tip of my chin.

"I-I think—" The words I tried to utter were ceased with a tender kiss. My mouth went still, processing the moment, the time, and documenting the date. Was he really kissing me? The heartless monster, the man who I thought couldn't stand the sight of me.

I guess he felt my resistance because he pulled back. His gaze was asking for permission to proceed. There was no way in hell I was going to pass up this moment to get everything I'd been dreaming about. Throwing caution to the wind, I ran my hand down the center of his chest to get an idea of what lay beneath. I snaked my hands around his neck and gently pulled him down to my 5'6" height.

At first, I teased his mouth with feathery kisses, savoring the moment. But then something stirred heavy in my belly, and I had to have him now. I caught his mouth in a sweet, yet rough kiss. Taking over, he turned my neck, angling my face to give him better access. I roamed my hands over his ass and he clutched one of my breasts, palming it as his mouth met my neck to kiss down the side of my collarbone.

Fuccck! We were getting our freak on in a tiny ass restroom. But I didn't give a damn as my mouth sought his out again, and our tongues found a rhythm as if they'd been familiar with each other.

Without notice, Agent Hawks picked me up and my legs instantly wrapped around his waist as he carried me over to a small bench sitting near the window. He sat down and placed me on top of him. This was a good dick riding position. I couldn't get all of what I wanted today, but maybe I could temporarily ease my urges. As I felt the length of him growing and pressing against my core through the thin leggings I wore, I rotated my hips. He pulled down the strap on my tank top and his mouth found my nipple. When he clamped down on my bud, I let out a loud moan as my head fell back.

I knew I had to be dreaming. There was no way that this was happening to me. However, reality kicked in fast when we both heard loud voices moving toward the door.

I hopped off his lap and pulled my tank top strap upward. Smoothing my hair back, I glanced around the bathroom and back at Agent Hawks still down on the bench with his dick standing at attention through his jogging pants.

"Do something with that," I said nervously. Running toward the door to lock it, I started to panic.

"What you want me to do?" he asked, trying to pull his waist-length shirt lower. "It won't go down."

Shaking my hands, I paced the length of the checkered black and white tile. "I'm going to get fired. This was a big mistake. I like you and all, but this was very careless of me," I rattled out.

Agent Hawks grabbed me by the swing of my arm as I began to make my sixth lap in the small, confined space. "It's going to be okay," he said calmly. "No one is getting fired." He rubbed my cheek.

A knock on the door had me jumping back from him. "Sky, are you in there?"

"That's Bella," I said in relief. "I'll steer her away and you can come out in like three minutes." I looked at him for confirmation.

Instead, he pulled me to him and lowered his mouth. Turning my head, I snatched my arm out of his grasp. "This shouldn't have ever happened," I said. "I have everything to lose."

"Sky! Are you in there?"

"Yes," I called over my shoulder.

I turned back around to face Agent Hawks. He placed one hand in his pocket and rubbed the back of his neck with the other. "You're right, Sky. This was my fault. I'm sorry."

Bella banged again on the door. "If you don't open up, I'm going to drop kick this door."

I swallowed the lump in my throat as I walked

toward the door. Opening it, I glanced back over at Agent Hawks before walking out.

He called me Sky. He never called me that before. With that last thought, I led Bella away from the bathroom and down the hall.

CHAPTER 5

KAREEM

*M*y number one rule was not getting involved with a coworker. The second rule was … well, there wasn't a second rule. My number one rule was the same for rule number two and three. *So, why did you do it?* That was the monopolizing question of the day. Slamming down the shot glass of whiskey on the bar top, I blew out a long breath.

"Bruh, you're going to break the countertop," Ant laughed.

I grumbled and took a swig of my beer that I'd been nursing for the past hour. Rubbing my forehead, I placed my elbows on the bar top and stared at the mirror behind the bar. I'd lost control, plain and simple. When Sky's full curves fell on top of me in the ring, something inside of me unleashed. I was no longer in control. Her warm heat pressed against my dick sent a fiery blaze coursing through my veins.

"I just can't believe I let it get that far," I said. I had

told Ant everything about what happened two weeks ago in the bathroom at the facility. I leaned in to whisper, "I had no business following her to the bathroom. It was like something came over me. Before I knew it, I was placing one foot in front of the other and then I was standing behind her in the women's restroom."

"You're human," Ant said, "You found her attractive and it happened."

I groaned again. "It shouldn't have never fucking happened." I lifted my head toward the ceiling at Mike's bar.

"I'm glad you finally lost control. You were too predictable, always following the rules." Ant looked my way with his drink halfway to his mouth. "Ninja, I was worried about you."

I lifted an eyebrow. "Ninja," I repeated. "Is that a new way of calling me a nigga?"

Ant chuckled. "Yep, you never liked the word, so I had to make it classy for you."

I couldn't help rolling my eyes. We were at Mike's Bar, which was located across the street from the FBI headquarters. It was our old hangout spot. We used to hit this place up every Saturday and Sunday night, after partying all night in the clubs or dissing some babe we met. It hadn't changed that much. The many flat screen televisions still hung around the room, and a few bar tables lined the length of the windows.

Mike was a huge Chicago Bears fan. He had the team colors of white, orange, and blue sprinkled throughout the bar. Also, there were a few Hall of Fame players' jerseys hanging from the wall. Like Walter Payton, Dick Butkus, and Bronko Nagurski to name a few. It was such a disrespect to the California teams. He didn't care what any Valley person had to say about his hometown. He was from the Windy City. I had once teased him that if he brought those sorry ass Bulls jerseys in this place, he was going to lose a loyal patron.

"Hey, man, did you hear me?" Ant asked.

Shaking my head, I turned his way on the swivel barstool. "Sorry, just thinking about how long we've been coming to Mike's Bar."

Ant nodded. "Yeah, it has been a long time, but you have bigger issues than Mike's Bar right now."

"I know, man," I confessed. "What am I supposed to do about it?"

Ant rubbed the bridge of his nose as if he was deep in thought. "You going to tell her how you feel?"

I paused, with my drink halfway to my mouth, giving Ant the side eye. "You want me to do what?"

Twisting his lips, Ant smacked the countertop. "You're going to have to take the lead on this one, Kareem, if you want to get anywhere with this girl."

I was already shaking my head before Ant got out the last word. "That's not going to happen," I responded. "Let me explain something to you." Leaning forward, I held my beer bottle in my hand. "For one, I'm pretty sure Sky thinks I'm the scum of the earth. Yes, I know she let me kiss her. But, man, you should've seen her reaction afterwards."

Ant raised an eyebrow. "Enlighten me."

Taking a swig of my beer, I leaned back on the barstool. "She said it was a big mistake and it will never happen again. I mean, dude, you should have seen her face. She was repulsed by me." I shook my head. "I'm even surprised she let me kiss her after I called her a maggot."

Ant spit the beer he was drinking across the bar. I slipped a few napkins his way as he hurriedly dabbed at the few droplets that squirted on the bar and his shirt.

"Ninja, you called her a what?" he asked.

"You heard me." I replied.

Ant grunted and focused his attention on the LA Rams playing against the Chicago Bears on the big screen television.

I shook my head and started scrolling through my Facebook page. To render Ant speechless meant there were nothing more to be said. I was a lost cause when it came to women. Mercedas proved that I couldn't get it right.

"Agent Starks and Agent Hawks." We both lifted our heads to our commanding officer, Agent Walks.

"I'm glad I found my two best agents here," he said, sitting on the barstool next to me.

I cleared my throat. "Sir."

He pulled out a manila folder from underneath his arm and called over the barmaid. "A shot of Jameson," he ordered.

Ant and I both gave him our full attention. Agent Walks was close to retirement from the bureau. He was in his sixties and had salt and pepper hair. He was my drill sergeant when I first started at the bureau. He was a hard ass known to push people to the limits. For him to discuss business inside of a bar must've meant it was serious. Finishing off my beer, I placed the glass on a stack of cocktail napkins in front me.

"We have a sting operation that we need you both on immediately," Agent Walks stated, getting straight to the point. "There is a new gang in town forming on 18th Street in the South Bay area." He paused and swallowed the shot the barmaid placed in front him. Coughing, he continued. "The FBI has been tracking this gang from state to state. We need to finally bring these criminals down before they catch whiff of us and move on. I need agents on surveillance, and we need a few agents to get in on the inside." He looked between Ant and I, and whispered, "Gain their trust, infiltrate their operation."

He fetched a pink bottle out his jacket pocket and took a swallow. Setting the Pepto Bismol on the countertop, he muttered, "Ulcers, it comes with the job."

I'd seen Agent Walks down two bottles of that pink stuff in one day. Hopefully, by the time the stress of the job kicked in for me, I'd be retiring.

He opened the manila folder. "Agent Starks, I need you on the inside. We have a few other agents who will join you, but we'll still be short. I've selected a few new recruits to join you."

I raised an eyebrow. "Sir, they haven't graduated yet?" I reminded him.

He raised a hand to silence me. "I know that, Hawks, which is why I've chosen the best, based off their merits and scores. I've taken into consideration their aptitude test, defense skills, and physical fitness." He locked eyes with me. "If you feel they aren't ready, just say the word."

Darting my eyes across the room, I replied, "No, my recruits are ready."

"Great." He flipped through a few pages and ran a finger down the white piece of paper. "Starks, you will have Lopez, White, and Norris."

He eyed me. "Hawks, you will run surveillance." Flipping to another page, he said, "Gomez, Miller, and," he paused, "Johnson will be your crew."

My mouth slightly gaped open. *Johnson and I in a tight ass room?* This must be my lucky day. But I couldn't deny the fact that she was ready and one of my best recruits.

He closed the folder and stood. "Your teams are being notified as we speak. Everyone is to report to the bureau at sixteen hundred hours to be briefed." He snapped his fingers and turned back around. "Hawks, the remainder of your class has been reassigned to Agent Pierce, until further notice." He closed the folder and stood. While rubbing his scruffy beard, he stared at one of the flat screens and grunted. After slapping a ten-dollar bill on the hard, black, bar top, he trudged out of the bar without a word.

"Damn!" Ant voiced, as soon as Agent Walks was out of ear range. "He just came in here and turned our good afternoon drink into a dud." He pushed his beer away. Frowning, he said, "I don't even want this shit no more."

I smirked, knowing exactly how Ant felt. I loved my job of being an agent. But the one thing I hated was the inconsistent schedules. I could be pulled out of my bed in the wee hours of the morning or be on a case for over a year. That's why having a wife and social life was hard to maintain. Most of the guys at the bureau were working on their second or third marriage. Ant was the only person I knew who still was married to his college sweetheart.

"Let's get to moving." I stood. "I have to go home and pack some stuff. Ain't no telling how long this operation will last."

Starks placed a few dollar bills on the bar and slapped my shoulder. "Now I have to go home and tell Shelly I'm about to be gone for a while." He grumbled,

"Man, I really don't want to hear her mouth. She had planned for us to go to Florida after Thanksgiving."

Snatching my FBI vest from the bar, I slid it on. "I told you, Ant, when you got married that the job was your first wife, and Shelly was—"

Ant sliced his hand in the air. "Don't start that shit, Kareem," he warned. "I already know what you going to say. But while you're over here all in my business, what're you going to do about Sky being on your team?"

"Ha!" I said, opening the glass door for Ant to walk out first. Shielding my eyes from the bright sun, I turned around to face him. "That's my business."

Ant chuckled and ran across the street to his car. "Aight, I'm out," he yelled over his shoulder.

Throwing up the peace sign to Ant's fleeing back, I made my way around the corner from Mike's Bar to the enclosed garage. Popping the locks to my truck, I flopped in the grey leather seats and laid my head against the head rest. Shit, what was I going to do about Sky being on my team? I mean, my life couldn't suck ass that bad. But it did unfortunately. Maybe this sting operation would give me the opportunity to apologize. Maybe show her I'm not the asshole everybody thinks I am.

Banging the palm of my hand against the steering wheel, I pulled out of the garage and into the busy California traffic. I had no training in this shit. Being nice and doing the right thing was a foreign language to me. However, something inside of me told me Sky was worth it. She was worth me taming the heartless monster and showing her the other side of Kareem.

CHAPTER 6

SKYLAR

The sound of a bottle hitting my carpeted floor woke me from my slumber. I popped open my left eye and the sunlight was shining bright through the window. Moaning, I slung my arm across my face to block out the annoying brightness. Something was licking my toes as I realized I was wrapped in a cocoon in my yellow comforter. Rolling in the bed, I attempted to peel the cover from my body. But the harder I tried, the more entangled I became. "Dammit!" I screamed. Lucky, my cat, made a hissing sound and skirted off the side of the bed onto the floor.

Freeing myself from the tangled mess of covers, I put my feet on the floor, and stepped on the bottle I heard hitting the floor. Placing my head in my hands, I remembered I had drank the whole bottle of vodka last night. And now Lucky was licking the rim.

"C'mon, stupid cat," I whined. "I don't want you to be a drunk, too." Picking up the bottle, I staggered into

55

my kitchen, wearing nothing but a black tank top and black panties. I threw the empty bottle in the trash and popped a Keurig cup in the coffee maker. Rubbing my eyes, I squinted at the clock on my microwave, which revealed that it was three o'clock in the afternoon.

"You have to be shitting me," I said aloud. I had slept the day away. Going through my family's photo album last night had brought back so many unwanted emotions. My mother holding me as a baby, my father and I going on our first fishing trip. And then there was Agent Hawks. *Ugh*, I thought, *I'm crazy about that man.* I was reckless and careless when it came to him, and I had worked too damn hard to lose it all to an office romance. *But that kiss!* I rubbed my lips, still feeling the aftereffects of his lips on mine.

He has a girlfriend, I had to keep reminding myself. *That didn't look all that hot either,* the devil on my shoulder added.

The beeping sound coming from the living room alerted me that my cell phone battery was dying. Taking my coffee mug with me, I realized it wasn't my personal cell phone beeping but my work phone. Picking up the phone from the wooden table, I saw I had a missed call from the agency. My heart skipped a beat, because this phone never rang, and the last I was told, calls wouldn't start coming through until after graduation.

I redialed the number and held my breath.

"Agent Johnson," the baritone voice said from the other end.

"Yes-s-s, this is J-Johnson," I stammered.

"You need to report to headquarters in sixteen hundred hours and be dressed in full uniform."

"Yes, sir."

When I heard the click of the phone hanging up, I let out a heavy sigh. *I'm about to get fired.* It was a Saturday and there was no need to come in the bureau. Unless someone found out about Agent Hawks and me.

Wait. There's nothing to find out.

What about the kiss and dry humping y'all did?

Nobody knows about it.

But what if he told someone?

Biting my fingernail, I shook my head. I couldn't believe I was having an argument with myself in my head. "He's probably not even thinking about my ass." Making my way into the bathroom, I turned on the shower and peeled my tank top from my sweaty skin. I was going crazy on what ifs.

I had other matters to attend to now. Like brushing my teeth, pouring a full cup of spearmint mouthwash in my mouth, and gargling for several seconds to dilute the smell of liquor on my breath. Next, I needed to do something with the heap of messy curls on my head.

Hurrying through my shower, I only washed the major parts. Once I was done, I moved around my loft like a tornado. Everything was in disarray. Clothes and shoes were on the floor of my bedroom and windowsill. I lived like a slob. My life spiraling out of control. I picked up my blue bra from the floor and smelled it. "It'll do," I said, as I snapped it in place, behind my back.

Snatching my work uniform from my walk-in closet, I hurriedly slid on my pants and button-down shirt. I grabbed my emergency tote bag of toiletries just in case and headed toward the door.

"Hey, what's up, Teegan?" I said, locking the door to

my loft. She lived a few doors down from me and was hauling what seemed like grocery bags in her hands.

She swung her long dreads over her back. "Oh, hey, Sky. Why didn't you come to the building meeting today?"

"Oh shit, Teegan, that was today?"

She nodded.

"I totally forgot about it, but I still need that massage from you. Hit me up when you have time," I hollered over my shoulder, while getting on the elevators.

Frowning, Teegan mumbled something under her breath. It didn't matter what she said. I was sure she wouldn't pass up a paying customer. *But I'll probably have to go to one of those stupid ass meetings before she gives me a date,* I thought.

&

Flopping down in the last vacant seat in the front row, I glanced around the classroom at the other agents. There were only five other recruits from my class that I remembered sitting in various spots. The expressions on their face resembled mine—scared shitless and wondering why we were here. The other agents and offi-cers were seasoned. They had been on the job for at least two to three years, which made me become uneasy. Everyone was dressed in their field gear. FBI jackets, cargo pants, and combat boots.

Leaning back in my chair, I folded my hands and took in slow, steady breaths to ease my nerves. The room instantly became quiet as I heard the trudging sound of boots coming from behind me. Agent Walks passed me and stepped in front of the chalk board, and a few other commanding officers came to stand behind him. And then Agent Starks and behind him was Agent Hawks. My breathing became heavy as I dropped my eyes to the white, long table.

"Listen up!" Agent Walks said. "We've assembled two teams to run detail. There is a gang arising in the South Bay area. Some of you will be working to get in the inside. That means you must think and act like a gangster. This gang is smart. They don't let anyone into their organization, without doing something illegal." He paused and eyed the class. "The second team will be on surveillance. You will record and listen to everything coming in and out of this area. Agents Hawks and Agent Starks will be taking the lead on this case. Everything will run through them."

Squirming in my seat, I sat forward. Agent Hawks looked my way, and I diverted my eyes to the white chalkboard.

"Now this brings me to our new recruits ..." Agent Walks paused and pulled out a clipboard. "Johnson, Lopez, Norris, White, Miller, and Gomez. You six are here because this is what you've been trained for. You're the best. Your commanding officer believes you're ready."

Yes! Excitement flowed through me as I imagined myself doing fist pumps in the air. *I finally get a chance to prove that I belong here.*

Diverting my eyes to the right side of the room, I saw Agent Hawks' eyes were fixated on me. I wanted to look away but couldn't, so we did this awkward stare down. Until Agent Walks clapped his hands. "This mission starts now. Let's go get the bad guys."

I stood quickly from my chair, throwing my duffel

bag over my shoulder, side stepping a few agents to get out the door. Someone gripped my arm. I turned around abruptly to protest and was greeted with a stern gaze from Agent Hawks.

"We need to talk," was all he said, escorting me down the hall.

He opened his office door and ushered me inside. Before I could turn, he had backed me up in the corner. "I think we have unfinished business."

Nodding, I licked my lips. "Yes, I believe we do. But I don't think your girlfriend will like you all up in my grill."

"Girlfriend! Grill," he repeated. Shaking his head, he reached out to smooth a strand of my curls behind my ear. "That's cute."

Pointing my index finger in his face, I said, "Don't play with me. I'm serious. You just can't kiss me whenever you feel like it."

"That kiss should've never happened." He closed his eyes. "But I'm drawn to you and I can't explain it. I don't know what you're doing to me."

"It's surprising to hear you say all of this, when all you do is give me shit. You even called me a maggot," I reminded him.

"I know ..." He took two steps back from me.

I shook my head. He wasn't about to be let off that easy. "You've been a dick to me and everybody in our class. You push us to our limits, and you belittle us. You're driving me crazy."

"I'm driving *you* crazy?" He smirked. "I have no clue how I'm going to run this sting operation with you being so close to me. How the hell am I supposed to keep my hands and eyes off you?"

Shrugging my shoulders, I walked toward the door. All of what he was saying sounded like his problem and not mine. Kareem was a distraction and something I needed to put far behind me.

"I'm not sure what to tell ya. It sounds like a *you* problem."

He grabbed my hand and brought his face mere inches from mine. "It sounds like an *us* problem."

My mouth became parched. I needed some water. Preferably a jug would do. He was eyeing me with those beautiful eyes again. And gosh, only if he knew what they did to my senses. Finding my voice, I said, "I need you to back up."

Just when I thought I'd broken through to him, he swooped down and caught my lips in a mind-blowing kiss. This time he didn't ask for permission. Thrusting his tongue inside of my mouth, he sought out what he was looking for. When our tongues started to do their familiar dance, I braced myself by curling my arms around his neck. Not feeling satisfied I was close enough, I stood on my tiptoes to gain better access.

Huge mistake! Kareem lifted me off the floor and carried me over to the edge of the desk. His hands were roaming all over my body. They landed on my ass, my hair, my back, and then on my face.

I broke away from the tender kiss to breathe. "I can't do this." Those words were short lived, because Kareem's mouth was back on mine—drinking from me like a thirsty man.

A knock at the door had us both jumping upright. *Damn, I always seem to get myself in these unexplainable situations with him.*

Starks popped his head through the door. He looked

back and forth between us, and said, "The team is gearing up in the combat room. We're all waiting for your instructions."

Kareem nodded. "I'll be there in five."

Starks smirked at me before closing the door.

Frowning, I turned to face Kareem. "You're going to make me lose my job," I huffed, moving toward the door again.

"You're not going to lose your job," he replied nonchalantly. Walking over to a small closet in the corner, he retrieved a handgun and stored it in the back of his pants. "I'm your commanding officer and any firing has to come through me."

Rolling my eyes heavenward, I reached for the doorknob.

"This isn't over," Kareem blurted behind me.

It is for me, I thought as I slammed the door. Jogging down the hall to the combat room to suit up, I had a knowing feeling that he was right. *We* were far from over.

CHAPTER 7

KAREEM

"*D*o you have to sit so damn close to me?" Sky whispered.

Smiling, I observed her squirming in the seat across from mine, and it made me want to laugh out loud. I had purposely sat next to her in the safe house we had setup for surveillance. The white house was simple—three bedrooms with computers and camera equipment in each room. Three cots were stashed throughout the house for rotating shifts.

"In fact, I do," I told her, watching as she rolled those big, brown eyes my way. Eyeing her up and down, I couldn't help but notice she was a beautiful woman. She wasn't scared to tell me when I was being a jerk, which was ninety percent of the time. She didn't grovel at my feet. And she didn't take my shit but dished it back at me. Those attributes were very sexy. *Damn!* I sucked my teeth. When her curly hair fell in her face, I had an image of myself fisting a handful of those curls, while I thrust inside of her sweet, tender core.

We were currently set up in the living room and Sky was ignoring me. She didn't know me well, if she thought I was the type of man to sit idle and let something I wanted pass me by. *When did you realize you wanted her?* Scratching my head, I had no clue on when my lust attraction towards Skylar turned into a forever thing.

"Hawks!" Agent Fox shouted from across the room.

"Huh?"

He walked toward me. "I said, Parker and I are about to take a lunch break and make a coffee run. Did you and Johnson want anything?"

Nodding, I replied, "Yeah, bring me back a large, black coffee."

"Actually, I'll go with you two," Sky said, grabbing her jacket from behind her chair.

Standing abruptly, I dropped the stack of papers in my hand. "You can't go, Johnson," I blurted, bending down to retrieve the scattered papers.

Frowning, she asked, "Why not?"

Think fast. "Someone has to keep their eyes on these monitors, and I have all this paperwork to fill out." I held up the large stack of papers.

She glared at me and then back at Agent Fox. Pursing her lips, she told him, "I'll take a coffee with just cream."

Agent Fox nodded and walked out of the house with Parker on his heels.

As soon as the door closed, I wheeled her roller chair up to mine and braced my hands on both sides. "You can't get away from me that easy. I told you we have unfinished business."

She folded her arms. "And I told you I was done with this game between us."

I cupped the side of her face. "Sweetie, this is not a game."

"How can you say this is not a game? You don't know anything about me. You're walking around here like you're used to getting what you want. But I'm not to be toyed with, Agent Kareem Hawks."

Rubbing the side of my beard, I stood upright. She was right. I was used to getting what I wanted. Or I fought hard to get it. Sitting back down in my swivel chair, I asked, "Tell me something about yourself."

Sky smacked her lips and cut an eye my way. "And why would I do that?"

"Sky, right?"

Her eyes widened. "Yes, that's right," she confirmed.

"I'm genuinely interested in who the real Sky is," I replied, reaching across her to retrieve an ink pen from the cup holder. She gasped. Chuckling, I sat back and watched the monitors of a few agents working the block of 16th Avenue as drug dealers.

"Hmmm. What do you want to know?"

"Everything. Anything you don't mind sharing." I paused and locked her with a serious gaze. "I want to know what's your favorite color, what type of foods you like, what your parents were like, and how many boyfriends you've had."

She peaked an eyebrow. "You want to know about the men I've dated?"

Raising my hand, I stated, "Correction, I only wanted to know the ones who you actually considered your man."

Sky focused her attention back on the monitors.

"My favorite color is red. I like seafood and I hate vegetables. My father was a sheriff and killed in the line of duty. My mother …" She swallowed. "I found dead in bed at the age of sixteen."

Placing a hand on her thigh, I murmured, "I'm sorry to hear that."

She continued. "I've never had a boyfriend."

"I find that hard to believe," I told her, clicking a button on the keyboard to zoom in closer on the center monitor.

"I've dated people but could never commit." Smoothing a curl behind her ear, she got a faraway look in her eyes. "I just never allowed anyone to get close to me."

"Why not?" I asked.

She shrugged her shoulders. "I guess I didn't want them to see the real me."

Leaning in closer to her, I asked. "Who's the real Sky?" When she didn't answer right away, I assumed I'd gone too far with the questions. Sky remained silent, staring at the monitors as if she was in deep thought. Instead of waiting on her to respond, I began to talk about myself. "I don't have a favorite color, I'll eat almost anything except for beets. My mother left us when I was a small child." I reared back in my chair. "I was so young I can barely remember what she looks like anymore. She remarried and had two other kids with her new husband. My father was ex-military; we moved around a lot. He took on the role of mother and father."

She looked my way. "That's messed up."

Nodding, I couldn't believe I was sharing such intimate details with her. Besides Ant, nobody knew about my childhood. Or the lack thereof. I was being an open book with her, which scared the shit out of me, but at the same time, I felt a sense of calmness come over me. As if I could share my most private moments with her. "Sky, like you, I've never really had a girlfriend. Just a few people to pass the time with."

"What about that woman I saw you with a few weeks back?"

"Like I said," glancing her way, I smiled, "just a few people to pass the time with."

She placed a hand on my shoulder. "So, all this Mr. Tough Guy routine is just for the job?"

"Naw, sweetie." I turned in my chair. "I am a tough guy. I take my job very seriously."

"So why were you such a douche bag to me?" Standing, she started pacing the length of the floor. She stopped and turned my way. "You know I wanted to hate your ass. You made coming to work each day hard as hell."

I reared back in the chair and let a boastful laugh. "Douche bag. I think that's a first for me."

"I'm serious, Kareem. We're on first name basis now … right?"

"Right, I'm sorry." Rising, I shifted my weight to my right leg. "I had to be hard on you."

"Why?" she screamed.

"Because if I didn't, everybody in that class would've saw straight through me. They would've seen my one weakness."

"What is your weakness, Kareem?"

I stepped toward her and took her hands in mine. "You can't see it? You're my weakness, Sky. Ever since the day you walked into my class, I wanted you." Bending down, I captured her lips in a kiss. I felt her relinquishing all control as she melted against me. This was very reckless of me to be doing on this on the job. But with Sky being near, there was no way I could keep my hands off her.

She leaned her head back. "I'm your weakness?"

When I nodded, she pressed against me to wrap her hands around my waist. I gripped a handful of her curls and angled her mouth slightly to the right to deepen the kiss. I snatched my mouth from her lips to shower her neck and face with kisses. She panted breathlessly against me. Backing her up to the small cot in the corner, she fell against it, bringing me down with her. I laid on top of her, grinding my hips against her core and removing the few strands of hair from her face that were blocking her full lips. Finding my mark again, I roamed her mouth with the tip of my tongue. Teasing the corners as I dove back in for another fiery kiss.

"Kareem, you're driving me crazy," she uttered above a whisper.

I kept my grinding slow as I moved down to her big breasts, unbuttoning a few buttons to get to my two friends, which I had the pleasure of sampling not too long ago. Popping the left chocolate bud in mouth, I sucked as she squirmed against me. She reached down for my belt buckle.

"Not yet," I warned her. I wanted it to be clear what I was looking for with her. Not a woman to pass the time with, but a woman who I could share my deepest moments with. A woman who understood my line of work. And a woman I could call my own. However, although I tried to resist the tugging at my pants, I found myself reaching between us and unzipping her trousers. I eased my hand in her panties. "Shiiit," I hissed.

Sticking a finger inside of her tight core, I discovered she was very wet. She bucked underneath me, moaning uncontrollably. I stuck in another finger. This time she let out a squeal that had me kissing the side of her neck. As I moved my fingers in and out of her core in fast, uncalculated motions, she grabbed the side of my face. "I need you now."

"In time," I replied, moving down to her belly button, kissing circles around it. As I pulled her pants down her legs, I took her panties with them. Spreading her legs apart, I flicked my tongue against her clitoris. Loving the way, she moaned my name I repeated the action again and again. Soon, I buried my face between her folds and licked, kissed, and sucked gently on her bud.

"Is this what heaven feels like?" she asked in between breaths. "I can't take it any longer," she cried.

"You have to," I mumbled. "Your commanding officer orders it."

"Yes, sirrrrrr," she slurred.

I used my fingers to join in on the torture I was giving with my mouth. Feeling her body pulsate and shake underneath my mouth, I knew her release was near. So, I increased the speed of my fingers and bit gently down on her bud.

Sky locked her legs around my head and held my face in place as she sat forward on the cot and let out a heaving scream. Licking up the last drop of her sweet nectar, I sat back on my haunches.

She reached for my belt buckle, and I stalled her hands. "God knows I want this, but we don't have much time. You need to go get yourself together."

Pointing down to my manhood standing at attention,

she said, "I think you need to get yourself taken care of."

I smiled. "Yeah, you always do this to me."

Sky sashayed into the attached bathroom and closed the door. *Shit, how was I going to do my job, when my sole distraction sat only inches from me?*

Walking back over to the cameras, I checked on Starks and his team. I sighed; it seemed like everything was still the same. Agents still stood on the corners of the new gang turf. I scratched the crown of my head and took in a deep breath.

Hearing the front door unlock, I watched as Agent Fox came strolling in with three cups stashed inside of a carryout tray. "Any change?" he asked

I shook my head as Sky came out of the bathroom. Her eyes darted around the room as if Agent Fox and Parker knew what we had done minutes ago. She came next to me and rolled her chair back up to the desk.

Accepting the coffee from Agent Fox, she said, "Thanks."

Taking a sip of my black coffee and crossing my legs to hide my erection, I focused my attention back on the monitors. After what had just happened between us, I knew we couldn't keep the secret long. However, before the bureau found out about us, I hoped I'd get the chance to let her know how I felt.

CHAPTER 8

SKYLAR

Giving oral sex had to be Kareem's sexual advantage to get women. Not only was the man a master at kissing but ... that tongue of his should be labeled as lethal. I shook my head. If I had to stay in this safe house with Kareem any longer, I was going to fuck his brains out. Because I was dying to feel and taste that long pole between his legs. When he was grinding against me, I could've sworn he was inside of me. Closing my eyes, I could still feel the heat that was mounting between us. This must have been one of the reasons why people said don't date your coworkers or better yet, your boss. Especially when your boss looked like Agent Kareem Hawks' fine buff ass.

No one had made me come as hard and fast as he did today. After our little make out session, he thought he was smart by sitting next to me and wrecking my senses. But I was good at manipulation. Really needing a drink right now, I scratched my arm. If only I could find some privacy to get my bag and have a swallow. It didn't seem that was going to happen anytime soon. When Kareem turned and said we had one more day in the safe house, before our relief team would come, I blew out a long breath, hoping that the days would fly past.

"How long have you been living in Park Manor?"

Snapping from my reverie, I turned to face Kareem. "Ugh, a few months now. Why?"

He shrugged his shoulders. "I was just wondering, because a few agents live in that building and it's pricey." Holding his hand in the air, he backtracked. "I'm not saying you can't afford it."

Shaking my head, I agreed, "I can't afford it." I laughed. "I was able to snag the last un-renovated apartment in the complex. If you take one of those apartments the rent is cheaper."

"Okay, that makes sense. So, what's your favorite restaurant?"

Turning around in my chair, I saw Agent Fox and Parker were loading a few bullets in guns and talking amongst themselves. "I really don't have a favorite restaurant," I revealed. "Between the FBI training and trying to study for the tests it doesn't leave me much time to explore the city."

"Hmmm. I'm going to have to do something about that. Santa Monica is beautiful." He placed his hand over his chest. "And it's breaking my heart to hear you haven't seen it."

Shrugging, I whispered, "Well, I'm open to see it. We jumped too fast I believe. We skipped the courting part and went straight to the bedroom."

Kareem frowned. "What is courting?" he chuckled.

Shaking my head, I answered, "I'm sorry, it's a southern word that means going steady."

Kareem's frown deepened.

"It means dating."

"Oh," he said. "You're from Alabama, right?"

Nodding, I asked, "How do you know?"

He remained silent too long, as if he revealed something he shouldn't have. "How do you know, Kareem?" I asked again.

"You have to call me Agent Hawks," he corrected me with a wary gaze.

"Bullshit," I whispered. "Now we're back to formalities after the moments we shared?"

"We can't do this here," Kareem said and stood to walk over to the corner of the room, pressing some wires in the wall. I was right on his heels, not giving a damn who heard us. I needed answers from him. How much did he already know about me? The more people got close, the sooner they were to reveal my secret.

When I touched his arm, he spun around and yelped. "Recruit, I need you to watch the monitors."

Agents Fox and Parker stared our way in confusion.

My mouth gaped open and my eyes widened at the tone he was using with me. I wasn't naïve to think he would start treating me differently around others. But what I didn't think was he'd be so damn cruel about it. Taking my seat, I crossed my arms and legs. *Screw Kareem.* If he wanted to play this hot and cold game, then I could do the same. Pouting, I folded my arms as my eyes narrowed to slits and threw murdering daggers at Kareem's back.

&

"Oooo, a little lower," I instructed Teegan as she massaged my upper back in her shop. She was very in tune with her client's needs. She had lit a few incense and candles around the room. One of the lavender fragrances had begun messing with my allergies. I let off a round of sneezes.

"Are you okay?" Teegan asked, running to the side of the room to light another candle.

"Yes," I replied, wishing she would catch the hint that she had too much shit burning in the dungeon room.

Closing my eyes, I tried not to breathe as much.

"Relax your body, let the tension melt away," she said.

I did exactly what she said, as I felt her long dread-locks scrape across my lower back. Teegan was kind of weird to me, with her long skirts and many piercings. However, I learned long ago not to judge a book by its cover. I'm sure someone thought the same about me.

"You're not relaxed, Sky. I can feel you tensing underneath my fingertips."

Maybe I can't relax because I'm half-naked! "Okayyy, I'm relinquishing power, I'm relaxing."

"You have to believe if you want this to work."

Nodding, my mind drifted to two days ago being in that safe house with Kareem. After our argument, I hadn't talked to him since. One day he tried to corner me in the bureau parking lot, but I hopped in an Uber and directed Mo to speed right past him. Maurice aka Mo was like Park Manor's personal Uber driver. He was always servicing our area. I had gotten to know him well by being a resident at the complex. Not too many people had cars living in the city. There was really no need for one.

"Ouch," I squealed.

"That's a tense spot," Teegan stated. "I have to move down to the deep tissue to work the cramp out." I didn't know what she was talking about—deep tissues, cramps, it didn't matter as long as she could ease my rapid thoughts. Of course, I had to promise Teegan I'd attend one of those building meetings she's always holding. It didn't matter, I had every intention on attending to get this voting over with that she kept harping about.

"I'm going to leave you here for five minutes, Sky." She picked up a timer on the counter. "Once you hear this buzzer go off, you can get up and get dressed."

Moaning, I kept my eyes closed as I heard the click of the door. After waiting three minutes, I got up to start getting dressed. Five minutes was too long for me. I had better things to do. Like figuring out how much Kareem knew about me.

Walking back into the main area of the shop, I found Teegan talking to Burgundy. This girl was always dressed to impress, with her matching blue earrings, heels, and pantsuit.

"Hey, Sky," Burgundy said, eyeing me up and down.

"Hi, Burgundy!" I replied. Being around her always made me get a bad vibe. Like she knew me.

"I told you five minutes, Sky."

Raising my hand in defense, I smiled. "I know, Teegan. I remembered I have something to do."

She twisted her lips. "My methods are not going to work if you don't do what I tell ya."

Placing my purse strap on my arm, I told her, "I'll keep that in mind."

As I was making my way out of the shop, I heard Burgundy in the distance. "Hey, Sky, hold up."

Turning around, I said, "Hey, waz up?"

"How you been doing?" she asked.

I massaged the back of my neck. "I'm good."

"Look, I know this group that can help you." She pulled a white business card from her purse. "Give them a call."

Hesitating, I looked down at the card in her hand. "What am I supposed to do with this?"

She flipped her hair. "Get some help for your drinking problem."

"Who told you I had a drinking problem?" I asked. Burgundy was too damn close. Her knowing this information meant that she could blow my cover.

"Sky, I'm not here to judge you or anything like that. My mother had a problem with drinking. So, I know the symptoms. Dilated pupils, dark rings under the eyes, fidgety, and always on edge."

"Wow! Who made you Dr. Phil?"

"Whateva, Sky." She stuck the card in the side pocket of my crossbody purse. "I'm just trying to help."

With a wave of my hand, I dismissed her final words and made my way down the street. I hated when people got all up in my business. Was Burgundy way off base? Hell naw, she was right on target. If it was easy for her to see what I was, I just wondered how long it would take before my cover was blown at the bureau. Better yet, how long would it take for Kareem to discover the one thing I'd tried so hard to hide?

CHAPTER 9

KAREEM

I must've been out of my mind to do those things I did to Sky. Shaking my head, I had to admit it felt so good and right to feel her core pressed against my mouth. But that didn't excuse the fact that she was my recruit and the woman had an issue with taking commands. Slapping my forehead gingerly, I ran faster around the field track across the street from the bureau. It was a little bit after midnight and too late for any sane person to be jogging in the dark.

I'd already had a few people look my way who must've mistaken me for a kidnapper or some sexual predator because they started to walk in the opposite direction. I guess I didn't help their suspicion wearing a black skull cap pulled down on my forehead and a black hoodie with FBI printed on the back. Running had always helped me work out my issues with the world. But I only had one pressing issue and that was recruit Skylar Johnson.

Shaking my head, I ran faster, jabbing a few punches in the air. Today was Thanksgiving and soon people would be awakening to join their families for a feast. Which was something I wouldn't be doing, given the fact that my sister was stationed overseas, and my father was in a nursing home, suffering from dementia. My visits with him had lessened over the years. The more I became harder to recognize, I stayed away. I couldn't see his mind waste away like that.

My cell phone vibrated in my jogging pants. "Hawks," I shouted.

"The sting operation bust is going down at zero seven hundred hours," Agent Walks blurted on the other end. "I've already contacted your team. However, I can't get ahold of Johnson. I need you to make a house visit."

"Why me, sir?"

"That's your recruit, Hawks, and you vouched for her, remember?"

Nodding, I came to a complete stop and clicked the alarm blaring from my watch. "Well, I know where she lives but I don't have the full address."

"I'm sending that over to your phone now. And when you do link up with Johnson, make sure you let her know that not answering the bureau calls is considered unacceptable."

I ended the call with Agent Walks after assuring him that I would get in contact with Sky. It was a little after twelve thirty and too late to be making house calls. To add to that, Johnson and I really weren't on speaking terms. She wanted answers from me that I couldn't give without blowing my own cover—I was snooping in her background. But I wondered what she was hiding. She was so on edge, eyes damn near bulging from her head when I revealed she was from Alabama. I guess it wasn't uncommon for special agents to know their recruit's life history. However, if I divulged how I knew where she was from, it wouldn't take a genius to figure out I'd been in her file.

I took a shortcut to the parking lot, jogging across the fresh cut lawn to my truck. Hopping inside I checked my iPhone for the address. As promised, Agent Walks had sent Sky's address. Starting the engine, I leaned back against the grey leather headrest and closed my eyes. Praying was something I'd never done before. I wasn't quite sure how the act was performed. But Sky had me doing some unorthodox shit. Lifting my head toward the sky, I said, "Dear, Jesus. I mean, God, give me the words to speak to Sky. Don't let me make an a— oops, sorry, don't let me make a fool out of myself. And if this is the person I should be with, please give me a sign."

Opening my eyes, I peeled out of the lot and headed toward Park Manor. After cruising through the clear streets, I arrived in no time. Luckily, I found a spot in one of the visitors' parking spaces. Making my way inside, I was stopped by the doorman. "Excuse me, sir, all visitors have to be announced after midnight."

I didn't think Sky would let me up if she knew it was me, but I had come all this way and had to see my mission through. "Alright, I'm here to see Skylar Johnson." I checked my phone for the apartment number. "Ummm, apartment 4B."

The doorman nodded and pushed a couple numbers on the phone. After a few seconds he said, "I have a …" Placing his hand over the receiver, he asked, "Sir, what's your name?"

"Hawks." I rephrased it, "I mean, Kareem."

He relayed the message, and after a few seconds he hung up the phone. From the puzzled expression on his face, I was prepared to walk back to my car. Until he said, "You can take the elevator on the left. The other two are out of service during these late hours."

"Thanks." I stepped inside of the elevator and took it to the fourth floor. Taking in a deep breath, I made my way down the hall. Just as I raised my arm to knock on the door, it swung open to a bewildered Sky.

"Why the hell are you at my house this late?" she screamed, tying the strings to her short, silk robe she was wearing. A luscious boob snuck out of the thin material.

"Ummm …" I began and paused, my hand itching to reach out and touch temptation. "The bureau was trying to get in contact with you."

She raised an eyebrow. "Why?"

The door from across the hall swung open. An older, frail woman squinted her eyes and asked, "Skylar, are you okay? I heard screaming."

"I'm sorry, Mary, please go back in. I'm okay."

She wiped her eyes and looked between us two. "Well, okay, let me know if you need anything. That's a lot of man standing in front of you."

I frowned, and Sky interjected, "It's fine. I promise." She tugged me in the door by my sweatshirt. "Goodnight, Mary."

Chuckling, I took in the view of her quaint apartment. It was decorated with bold, bright colors—red curtains, yellow sofa, and burnt orange end tables. Nothing really matched but it seemed to all tie in together in some weird way.

"Why is the bureau trying to get in contact with

me?" she asked over her shoulder, while locking the door.

"Oh, the sting operation is going down at zero seven hundred hours."

Sky turned around. "Oh," she said, and checked the gold watch on her arm. "I have about five hours to get dressed." She glanced over at a glass sitting on the bar table. Running over, she grabbed it to pour down the drain. She looked back and forth around the apartment. "Well, I'll meet you there," she said nervously.

For the first time since entering Sky's apartment, I looked at her with new eyes. "Are you okay?"

She waved me off, moving toward her dishwasher, and started loading a few plates inside. "Why do you ask?"

I shrugged my shoulders. "I don't know, probably because of the way you're acting really fidgety and on the edge. And the fact you're loading damn dishes in the dishwasher at one in the morning."

"I'm fine, Kareem. I mean, Agent Hawks."

Rubbing my hand down my face, I tried to explain, "Look, I'm sorry about that day. Like I said, people can't know about us."

"There's no us," she corrected me. "Plus, it's time for you to leave."

"Are you sure that what's you want?" I asked, closing the distance between us. She was still facing the sink. I came close to her backside but didn't allow our bodies to connect. Leaning down, I whispered close to her ear, "You don't want to finish what we started in the safe house?"

She abruptly turned around, causing me to take a step back. "You don't get to just march up in here and take what you want." She jabbed a finger in my chest. "You may be my commanding officer, but don't expect me to fall at your feet. I mean, who do you think you are?"

She moved from my grasp and into the living room. "You expect me to pick up where we left off? Jump back in your arms and ease this hot attraction we have toward each other. Should I just fuck you so we can just move on from whatever this fucked up situation is we got going on?" She paused and looked my way.

I had my arms folded and a smirk covered my face.

"What's so fucking funny?" she asked.

"You," I stated firmly.

"How is anything I said, remotely fun—" Her words were cut off as I slipped my tongue inside of her mouth.

She moaned and fell against me. Our tongues greeted each other with their familiar twirls. She tasted so sweet and felt so soft. A waft of vodka invaded my nostrils. However, anyone who worked our career would need a drink from time to time. Wrapping my arms around her full waist, I pulled her against me. My mouth traveled down to her chin and ventured to her neck. She laid her head in the crock of my neck, kissing my earlobe.

"Why can't I say no to you?" she asked breathlessly.

"Maybe because your heart wants this?"

She pulled her head back and looked me in the eyes. "What about your heart?"

Blowing out a heavy sigh, I replied, "Tonight, it wants you."

"What about tomorrow?"

I didn't want to think beyond tonight. Pulling her

back to me, I lowered my head, "We'll figure it out tomorrow."

Those words must've been satisfying, because Sky kissed me with such a hunger, I could feel the heat radiating from her skin. She went straight for what she wanted. She rubbed her hands against my erection. That didn't ease her desires because she slid her hands down into my jogging pants and inside of my boxers. Finding what she was looking for, her breath hitched.

"Oh damn," she mumbled. "That's a lot to work with, Kareem."

I chuckled. "Like your neighbor said, I'm a lot of man."

Tucking her lips between her teeth, she punched my chest. "Well show me."

I lifted her in my arms and carried her toward the narrow hallway that I believed led to her bedroom. "Which way?" I asked as we came to two doors.

"To the left."

Kicking the door open, I sat her on the bed. "You don't know how long I've dreamed about this." Stepping back, I pulled the hoodie and t-shirt over my head.

&

SKYLAR

"Shiiit," I said. "I could tell you're buff, but your body is magnificent." Running a hand across his ripped eight-pack, I feathered a few kisses over each ab.

He growled, lifting his head toward the ceiling. Slipping his hands in my heap of curls, he massaged my scalp.

The act was driving me bananas. I pulled him closer to me, needing him bad and not in the way he probably thought I would take him first. Glancing at my nightstand clock, I saw it was a little past two o'clock. We had time. I eased his joggers down his strong legs and took in the view.

It was staring right at me. Beckoning me to swallow it whole. It was a lot to take in, but I was big girl and up for the mission. Taking in a deep breath, I peeked up at Kareem's face and he was watching me through lowered eyelids.

This is what you've been wanting. Giving in to my thoughts, I opened my mouth and eased his length inside, gripping it with my hand. He hissed. I created enough saliva to glide him in deeper. *Thank goodness I had my tonsils removed years ago,* I thought, as I slithered him down to the back of my throat. I gagged a little but kept twirling my hand and using my tongue to run the length of his dick.

"Shiiiit, Sky," he groaned.

Now both of his hands were in my hair, guiding my head back and forth. He pulled my head back, to where his dick was sitting on the tip of my lips. I twirled my tongue around the head of his dick and flicked it up and down.

"Fuck," he hollered.

Taking the length of him back in my mouth, I wanted to work him into a big nut. I tried to swallow him whole. I felt him tugging at my head, but I didn't let up. I kept my mouth in place and my hand working around the bit of dick that my mouth couldn't cover. I bobbed my head up and down his shaft.

"Easy, baby," he murmured. "I don't want to come right now."

"Uh huh," I said as his pleading fell on deaf ears.

"Oh shit," he yelled, pulling my head from his dick and taking a step back. "You like to disobey me," he remarked with a grin.

Smiling, I said, "Yes, sir," while watching a few droplets of cum drip from his dick.

"Hmmm." He pushed me gently on the bed by my shoulder, straddling me in all his nakedness. I marveled at his beefy body. I reached up to trace the connecting goatee he sported. I loved that shit. The Rock didn't have nothing on him.

He untied the belt to my robe and my titties sprung forward. I knew they were his favorite treats. Some men loved the ass, but Kareem was a breast man.

His phone rang. I frowned, pulling my robe closed. *Who could be calling him in the wee hours of the morning? Mercedas?*

Hurrying off the bed, he fetched the phone out the pocket of his joggers. "Hawks," he barked. "Yes, I understand, sir. Thanks for calling."

Ending the call, he turned my way. "It looks like we have all night."

"Huh?"

"Agent Walks said the sting operation has been postponed. Something about he's gathering more footage."

I inwardly smiled.

But without warning his eyes turned dark. He was almost unrecognizable as his face held a serious gaze. "I want you to understand, Sky, what's about to happen here." He paused. "I'm crossing the line in a big way and that's something I don't do. But I need you, I can't stop this." He pointed between the two of us. "I'm not sure what's happening here but I like it."

"I like it, too," I said, pulling his mouth down to mine. "There's too much talking and stopping going on," I confessed. My body needed this. As he wrapped his mouth around one of my mounds, my mind shattered into small pieces.

CHAPTER 10

KAREEM

She was right, there was too much stalling. We both wanted this, and there was no reason for us to continue to prolong the inevitable. I opened Sky's robe fully, getting a full scan of her body. She only wore a pair of lacy red panties. "I see you like bright colors."

She smiled underneath me as I kissed her neck, palming her breast at the same time. I reached down and slipped the thin material from her hips. Taking a quick waft of her scented panties, I tossed them to the floor.

"You're a freak, Kareem."

I laughed. "You have no idea, sweetie." Grabbing my wallet from the back pocket of my joggers, I fetched out a condom. Tearing it open with my teeth, I rolled it down my shaft.

Sky's eyes widened, and I smiled. "I'll go easy."

When she nodded, I placed her arms above her head. I spread her legs open with my knee and settled at her core, inching inside of her womanly folds. She gasped. My head fell to the crook of her neck. *Damn, she's so tight.* I thrust a little harder and she clutched my back. Pulling out a little, I drove to the hilt.

"Oooo," Sky moaned.

Rocking in and out of her core, she pooled with wetness. Her sweetness welcomed me, pulling me deeper inside. She gripped my ass cheeks, squeezing them hard as I lifted my head and let out a howl.

I was on the brink of busting one, but I didn't want to come just yet. I slowed my pace, and before I knew it, Sky had flipped me on my back, and she was easing slowly onto my dick. She braced her hands on my shoulders and rocked her hips back and forth, moaning uncontrollably.

Placing my hands on her hips, I attempted to slow her movements. It was no use because Sky started bouncing up and down on my shaft. I felt my toes curling and my eyes started to roll.

"I want you to hit it from the back," she stated.

&

SKYLAR

I waited until my words registered with Kareem as I hopped off his long dick and got into the doggy-style position. He took a handful of my hair and twisted it around his hand. Nudging my back in a deeper bend, he thrust inside of me from behind.

"Fuccck," I echoed through the room. I didn't think I even knew what I was asking for. I felt Kareem's dick in my stomach. Closing my eyes, I rode out the pain mixed with pleasure. He gently pulled my head back and drove deeper, his dick pulsating inside of my core. Flashes of bright lights bounced underneath my eyelids. My body fell to the bed as Kareem's pumps increased. He reached around to the front of my pussy and played with my clit.

The acts of his dick and hand stimulation were driving me insane. I clutched my pale blue sheets and gasped for air. Feeling my orgasm building damn near snatched my breath away from me. I bit my bottom lip as he increased the friction, nearly killing me in the process. My heart fluttered, and my legs went numb. I never imagined how I would die, but if this is the way the sweet lord decided to take me with good dick inside of me then I would be at peace with his decision.

"Ohhhh," I screamed. "Shit, fuck, I can't breathe, wait, wait," I mumbled. Out of nowhere, Kareem lifted his hips and hit something that shattered my flood gates. I felt the wetness oozing from my core and down my thighs. My body shook, sending me into a light seizure, I thought. All this good-feeling weird stuff was happening to my body and it felt soooo good. My heart fell from my chest and landed right in the palms of Kareem's hands at that moment. He gathered what was left of my limp body and placed me on his heaving chest.

I closed my eyes as I felt the cool sheets drag over my hot body. Reaching down to feel my legs, I discovered they were still attached but wouldn't move. I twisted my hips to snuggle deeper under Kareem's armpit and a gush of fluid ran from my core. *I can't believe I'm still coming.* Smiling, he kissed the crown of my head. It wasn't long before I heard a light snore escape his lips. Since walking or standing wasn't possible yet, I drifted off to sleep and hoped that I wasn't the only one tonight who had found their *forever*.

&

KAREEM

Opening my eyes, I quickly closed them from the bright sun shining from the window shade. Turning over on my side, I watched as Sky slept so peacefully. All the things we did in the early morning still invaded my thoughts. Her face was covered by her hair. I moved the few strands from her forehead and counted the brown freckles on her nose. "Six," I whispered. She was absolutely perfect. The sun highlighted the planes of her naked body.

The sheets had floated to the foot of the bed and her coke-bottle shape glistened underneath my gaze. I traced the brown chocolate chip birth mark on her hipbone with the tip of my finger. She squirmed in her sleep and I moaned at how soft her skin felt. Moving to the edge of the bed, I eased out. Bending down, I felt around for my socks. I reached under the bed and something licked my hand. "Shit," I blurted.

A meow came from under the dark space as a fluffy brown and white cat skirted pass me. "She has a cat." I frowned. *Where was his ass last night?*

Shrugging my shoulders, I reached my hand back under the bed, hoping I didn't get any more surprises. I grabbed a hold of what seemed like a bottle. I pulled it out. "A tequila bottle. Huh." I peeked underneath the bed and there were at least four other empty bottles rolling around. I pulled them out one by one. As I did, I read each of the labels. My stomach began to twist into knots. There were two vodka bottles, a bottle of gin, and a bottle of Remy Martin.

Frowning, I stood upward and glanced around the room. Her room was a mess. Clothes, shoes tossed around the floor, and drinking glasses lined her nightstand. My head started to swirl as I saw my socks piled by the closet door. Slipping them on my feet, I hurried and got dressed. Pulling my hoodie over my head, I heard, "Are you leaving?"

Pushing my arms through my sleeves, I frowned as my head peeked through the hole of the sweatshirt. "Yeah, I got to get out of here."

She sat upward in the bed, holding the sheets around her neck. "What's wrong?" she asked with furrowed eyebrows.

I picked up the liquor bottles from the floor. "What is this, Sky? Please don't tell me you had a party in your room. These bottles were freshly used. I can still smell the alcohol scents."

She shook her head. "You don't know me. So, don't judge me."

"You're right, I don't know, so can you explain? Because the way it looks now, it seems like you need some help."

She raised her hand. "I don't need this shit. You can get the fuck out, Kareem," she hollered.

I sat on the edge of the bed. "I'm not leaving without answers."

"What do you want to hear?" she screamed, slapping the bed. "Alright, will this get you to leave? I'm a fucking alcoholic, I've been drinking since I was sixteen years old, when I found my mom dead in the bed. I started drinking even more when my father died. There it is, my big fucking secret." She swatted at a few falling tears. "Don't pity me. You don't know how it feels to lose both of your parents and to be the only child and have no one in this world to talk to."

Placing her head in her hands, she sniffled.

"How did you pass the alcohol test and the lie detector test?" I inquired. I really needed to know the answers to these questions.

She lifted her red face from the palm of her hands. "My godfather is a retired FBI agent. The DUIs I couldn't get expunged from my record he wiped them out." She shrugged her shoulders. "Shit, I don't know all the other details, but he got me in. This agency was supposed to be a new start for me."

"That explains why certain parts of your file was locked." I shook my head.

"You were in my file?" She frowned.

I nodded. "Yes, that's how I knew you were from Alabama and it didn't reveal much. But now I know why. I just wanted to know more about you." I gazed toward the window at a few boats in the distance. "I needed to know about the woman I was falling for."

"You're falling for me?" she asked in surprise.

I continued to stare out the window without uttering a single word. My heart ached for her. Scratching my beard, I shrugged. "I was … I am. Shit, I don't know anymore." I blew out a long breath.

"You don't know?" she repeated more to herself than me.

I stood again as everything started to collide together in my mind. "I got to go," I said, placing my arms behind my neck to take a light stretch.

"So that's it? What about us? Do we go back to being the same as before?"

"You're my recruit, Sky. This type of information, I have to report."

She hopped out of the bed, her breasts bouncing with the sudden motion. She tied the sheet around her naked body. "Are you really about to report me? This is my life you're fucking with, Kareem. I divulged this information to the man I loved."

Those words had me looking up from the carpeted floor. "Love!" I repeated.

Grabbing my head in frustration, I said, "This all is a little bit too much for me. I follow the rules, I fucked up royally. I got involved with my recruit and I apologize for that." I pounded my head a few times with the palm of my hand.

"Yeah, I got to go." Picking my wallet up from the floor, I turned and made my way to the living room.

Sky was right on my back shouting at me, "You got involved with your recruit? That's what you think of me? After the night we shared and moments we spent. That's all I mean to you?"

I opened the door, and Sky slammed it closed. "Answer me, dammit."

Swinging around to face her, I got up in her face. "Sky, you're a mess. I hate to point out the obvious, but you are an alcoholic. You cheated and lied your way into the bureau. You deceived me into thinking you were somebody you weren't. I can't risk it all for someone who's not willing to change. Everything you've said out of your mouth thus far wasn't about how you were going to get help, but you made some way to make this all about me."

When her mouth gaped open and recognition rendered in her face, I turned on the heel of my shoes and slammed the door behind me.

Trudging to the elevators, I smashed the down button and groaned. Stepping inside, I laid my head against the panel wall. "Shit," I shrieked. I needed to head straight to the bureau and turn Sky in, but as I stepped out of the elevators and into the warm, Santa Monica air, my heart constricted. I couldn't do it. Like Ant said, I always followed the rules. I played everything safe. I only cared about myself. I wished that was the case now. Because there was another person who had crept their way into my heart.

CHAPTER 11

SKYLAR

I moved slowly around my apartment as I threw away the liquor bottles that Kareem had found hours ago. After I had cried myself to sleep and awakened to only cry myself asleep again. I had the urge to clean up my house for once. Picking up my dirty clothes from the floor, I placed them in the hamper stashed in the corner of the bedroom. I lined my shoes in the closet and cleared all the drinking glasses from my nightstand, tables, and bar top.

Kareem was right. I was a hot mess. Should I be mad at the words he spat at me? Maybe! But it was the truth. All these years I moved through life with a burden of guilt on my shoulders. I let my mother's death consume my life. Somehow, I thought it was my fault she died. Maybe if I was an obedient teen, or listened more or helped around the house, then she would still be here with me today.

Shaking my head, I realized it was time for me to get

ready for work. If I still had a job. I hadn't heard from Kareem or the bureau yet. Chances were he had a change of heart. I had to keep reminding myself that he was the heartless monster, and the night we shared meant nothing to him.

Feeling frustrated, I picked up my crossbody purse from the floor and a white card fell out of the side pocket. Plucking it up, I read the gold cursive writing on the front. *Alcohol Anonymous; its only membership requirement is a desire to stop drinking.* I twirled the card in my hand and walked over to my floor-to-ceiling windows. This was the card Burgundy had stuck in my purse weeks ago. A conversation with her was something I should have soon. Inhaling, I decided this program may be the first step I needed to get myself back on track.

My phone buzzed from the coffee table. Smiling at my caller, I cleared my throat. "Hey, Bella."

"Sky! You have to get down to the agency fast. Something big is going on."

My heart instantly dropped to the pit of my stomach. "What happened?" I blurted, running to my room to get dressed.

She whispered, "I don't know exactly, but it looks like some heavy shit and I saw your name on a white board."

Shit, I thought. "Okay, I'm on my way." Ending the call, my heart literally felt like it was about to beat out of my chest. I didn't know what was going on. And for my name to be on a board meant it wasn't good. I quickly said a prayer as I looked around my apartment hoping I didn't forget anything and praying to God I still had a job.

&

Slinging my duffel bag on my back, I rode the escalator up to the third floor. As I made my way down the hall, a few agents ran through the halls.

"Johnson!" someone shouted from behind me.

Turning slowly, I watched as Agent Walks stepped in my face. "We've been calling your work phone for hours and there was no answer."

"Oh m-myyyy g-goodness," I stammered, placing my bag on the tiled floor and rummaging through it for my phone. "Here it is." I pulled it out and noticed it was dead.

Agent Walks folded his arms. "Johnson, go suit up and meet in the tactical room ASAP. The sting operation is going down in the matter of hours," he screamed.

I guess I wasn't moving fast enough, trying to stuff my items back in my bag, because I heard a sudden growl. "Move it now, Johnson!" he shouted at the top of his lungs.

Hauling ass, I ran into the combat room and popped open my locker to stuff my bag inside. Strapping on my bullet proof vest, I cocked my Glock 22 handgun and placed it in my holster at my side. My left hand began to shake, and I smoothed it with my other hand. "C'mon, I don't have time for this today." I sometimes got the shakes. It was a sign of me not having my morning drink fix.

"You don't think you're going on this sting operation today?"

I turned around abruptly, slamming my locker in the process. "Kareem."

He stepped from behind the wall. He was dressed in

combat boots, black pants, and a shirt. And looked ruggedly handsome. Holding the straps of his FBI bullet proof vest, he stated, "You're not ready. I'm not letting you go to this operation and get yourself killed."

Dropping my gaze to the floor, I said, "You're right. I'm not well." I lifted my head. "But I know I can get better. Please don't blow my cover. Let me tag along, I'll fall back, stay low. I'll do whatever you say, Kareem." I swallowed. "Please."

He massaged the back of his neck and raised his head toward the ceiling. Blowing out a long breath, he sighed, "I can't."

At that moment my world shattered. This was it for me. Career gone down the drain, life in shambles, and the itch of drinking eating me alive. Reopening my locker, I yanked my duffel bag out. I ripped my name badge from my chest and threw it back in the locker. Cleaning out my personal items, I stuffed everything in my bag as tears welled in my eyes.

"Wait!" Kareem replied.

I stalled my movements with my hand holding the grey locker door.

"I hope I don't live to regret this, Sky." He punched the wall. "Suit up. You have to do exactly what I say," he growled through clenched teeth.

Nodding, I wiped away the tears and hoped I was truly ready for this mission.

&

KAREEM

My eyes darted around the safe house at the agents reviewing the layout of the blueprints of the gang members' drug house. Our safe house was stationed right across the street from the house we were going to hit. I cut my eyes to the left, where Sky stood three steps from me. I had ordered her to stay close. I could lose my fucking job for her. But damn, I had a strange feeling she was worth it. To see those tears streaming down her face this morning at the bureau seemed to wake up my heart.

She gazed my way with a smile that barely reached her eyes. I frowned and turned my head straight. Still leaning on one of the walls, Starks sent me a head nod, alerting me that the team was ready. I'd done many of these drug busts before. They could go good sometimes with no one getting hurt, or sometimes we brought back bodies.

I sent a head nod back to Starks and gripped Sky by the elbow. "This is what you signed up for. Stay close to me," I whispered. Walking to the center of the room, I cleared my throat, "Everyone has their post. The mission is simple … we hit quiet, fast, and get out alive. There will be shots blazing, we are taking them dead or alive." I swallowed, my eyes landing on Sky. Her lips were slightly opened, and her chest heaved rapidly. I continued. "Hopefully we can take more alive. Blue team, you're with me, and red team, you're with Starks." I paused for a second. "Let's get it."

Everyone cocked their guns and exited the front and back doors. I hated daytime drug busts, because everyone could see you coming. But it was the best time because that's when the drug dealers didn't expect it. I signaled for the left flank to move around to the back of the house. I turned around slightly, and Sky was right up under me.

Speaking through the wire of my shirt, I instructed, "Move in." It all happened so quickly. Doors being broken down, screaming, gang bangers running, shots being fired, babies crying, and women yelling. It was a blur as I held Sky by the arm. We moved through the house slow but quick. Most of the gang bangers were already in handcuffs laying on the floor as we made our way through, looking for money, drugs, or anything that was illegal.

A gunshot ricocheted in the room, and I quickly grabbed my chest and tumbled over to the floor. I gazed at the corner of the room and saw a kid, who looked barely thirteen holding a gun. Blinking once, another gunshot rang out in the room and the boy dropped to the floor. Glancing upward, I saw Sky standing holding her gun outward. She was frozen and breathing hard. I felt myself slipping in and out of consciousness. Before I knew it, everything went dark.

&

SKYLAR

Happy! That was the best word to describe how I was feeling now. Watching Kareem sleep, I realized it was time to change his bandages. Thank goodness, he only got shot in the shoulder. The doctor said if it was a little more to the left, it could've hit one of the main arteries. As I was peeling the soiled bandage from his arm, he jolted awake.

"What are you doing?" he asked in a groggy voice.

Laughing, I told him, "You needed your bandage changed."

"Hmmm," he moaned. "That's why I have a nurse." He blinked his eyes sleepily. "Did you go to therapy today?" he asked.

I set the bandages and ointment back on the end table and stood. I had been going to therapy at the bureau. I was ordered to do so, after shooting someone. Luckily, the poor boy didn't die. But that was the first time I'd ever shot anyone. It wasn't the same as shooting a deer, bears, or pop cans. It was someone's life I had in my hands. When I saw Kareem hit the floor, I just pointed and shot. I didn't think, I reacted. After that day, I really wondered if I was ready for this agent life. However, after attending classes of other first-time shooter offenders, I realized it was natural to feel this way. And I was exactly where I needed to be. I also enrolled in AA classes to get help for my drinking. "Yes, I went," I finally answered, rubbing my hands together.

"Good, the initial shock of shooting your gun will wear off soon," Kareem said nonchalantly.

Nodding, I leaned against the wall in Kareem's bedroom. It had only been two-weeks since the incident and we hadn't really had the time to talk about *us*. Since we were both were on medical leave, I'd stayed by his side day and night.

"Sky."

I glanced up. "Yeah," I said, sitting on the edge of the bed.

"I've never gotten around to thanking you for saving my life." He paused. "I was wrong. You do belong here. I always knew you did," he grumbled, trying to roll over on his left side to face me. "But I also knew you doubted yourself. And in this job, doubt will get you killed."

I smiled. Even when he was laying up in a bed and could barely move, he was still trying to be my commanding officer. "Yes, sir," I barked.

He chuckled. "Come here." The smile he held moments ago disappeared from his face. The serious Kareem gaze returned—deep scowl, creased forehead, and furrowed eyebrows.

Holding my breath, I slid my body closer to him.

"I love you," he said.

I paused. "Say what?" I asked.

He placed his hand on the side of my face and raised up from the bed. "I've never told anyone those words before. So, I hope I'm doing it right. I love you, Agent Skylar Johnson."

Smiling, I hugged his neck. "Yes, not Y-O-U-R recruit any longer." I giggled.

We both laughed in unison.

"I love you, too," I replied, placing a peck on his lips.

"That's all I get?" he grumbled.

Placing a finger on my cheek, I smiled. "Hmm, let me think about that."

"Think about this," Kareem said, pulling me on top of him and removing my green tank top. "Why do you like bright colors?" he asked, kissing a trail from my neck down to my breast.

Lifting my head, I laughed. "Sky is my name, and rainbows are bright, vibrant colors, right?"

Kareem didn't respond, but instead, popped one of my nipples in his mouth.

"Oooh," I moaned. Gasping in between breaths I said, "I always want to live my life like I'm in the sky riding on the high of rainbows. Dammmn, baby." I squealed when Kareem switched to my other boob, giving it equal pleasure.

"What else?" he asked.

"Because the sky is the limit," I blurted, reaching between us to glide his thickness inside of my wet, womanly folds.

"Shit," he hissed.

Clutching the sheets on the side of me, I rode Kareem's dick like it was the end of the world. Bucking my hips back and forth like a wild horse. He buried his face in my boobs. "Say it," I demanded.

He growled and gritted his teeth. "Yes, sir." I let out a round of giggles as Kareem rammed into me, erasing the laughs from my mouth and had me holding on for dear life. I was sure the neighbors in his building could hear me screaming his name at the top of my lungs.

The last thing I heard before my orgasm overtook me is, "You better eat your Wheaties the next time you want to play games with your commanding officer."

EPILOGUE

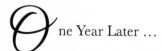ne Year Later ...

KAREEM

"Oh my goodness, bae. I don't think I can go to another restaurant," Sky whined, rubbing her swollen belly. "You've already taken me to three today and I can't even swallow water right now."

Chuckling, I glanced over at her sitting in the passenger seat. The pregnancy glow looked good on her. I wanted to keep my promise on showing her the finer restaurants that California had to offer. However, I didn't think we'd be doing it with a child on the way.

We both weren't ready. We thought we were taking the necessary precautions to prevent mishaps like this. But I guess God had other plans. Sky hadn't had a drink in a year. I was so proud of her for taking charge, and now she was a facilitator at the AA meetings leading other people to sobriety.

"Where are we?" Sky asked, staring at the multi-level complex I had just pulled in front of.

I leaned into to her and smiled. "I want to introduce you to someone."

She glanced from me to the complex. "Who?"

"My father."

Her eyes watered and she pulled me into a long hug. I had eventually told her about my father's dementia and how I had stopped visiting him. The truth about me was I ran from things that were hard or reminded me of my dad. Like how I ran from Sky when I deemed her not as perfect as I'd hoped. I didn't face my issues and I hid behind my work. It took me six months in therapy to admit those things about myself.

Sky wasn't the only one who needed help. I had to come to terms with my own shit as well.

"What are we waiting for? Let's go see your father." She hopped out of the car and wobbled her way to the entrance. Once we arrived at his room, he was sitting in a recliner with his back toward the door. I paused in the doorway, nerves and fright overtaking me.

Sky nudged me forward. "Go on."

I walked around the chair and stood in front of my father. It took a minute, but he finally raised his head, our eyes connecting at the precise moment. "My Kareem came back," he stated.

Falling to my knees in front of him, I cried in the palm of my hands. Sky placed a hand on my shoulders. Standing, I hugged my dad and said, "There's someone I want you to meet."

He smiled.

"This is Sky, my girl, and the one hiding in her belly is your grandson."

Sky's eyes watered with unshed tears. Getting on a knee in front of her and my father, I pulled a black box from my pocket.

She gasped, bringing a hand to her mouth.

"Will you marry me?" I asked.

Sky fell to her knees and wrapped her arms around my neck. "Yes, a thousand time yes," she cried.

Surprisingly, my father let out a laugh and started clapping his hands. In a loud voice he said, "The Hawks men are finally together again."

The End

LET'S STAY IN TOUCH!

I hope you enjoyed Her Forbidden Fantasy! I enjoy hearing from readers and would like to thank you in advance for any reviews, messages or emails.

Save and Author! Leave a Review!

Instagram: @sealsangie

Email: angelde.amor@ymail.com

Facebook: facebook.com/authorangelaseals.write

WOMEN OF PARK MANOR

Each novella in the Women of Park Manor series can be read in any order. See below for a list of all the books in the series.

INVITATION TO BID

When Nicholas Brown gets a call from Mama Peaches to come back home for a neighborhood bachelor auction, he doesn't want to do it. But who can say no to Mama Peaches? As a surgeon known for taking calculated risks for big rewards, he lives his life fast, crazy and on the edge. To save himself from the claws of women placing bids at the auction, this bachelor comes up with a scheme… Despite how things ended, Nick has always held a torch for his beautiful, former high school sweetheart, Raina Lawson. So, who better to bid on him than a woman he trusts? She's a safe bet, which makes her the best bet!

After high school graduation, Nick left her high and dry without any real explanation. And now, the impressive doc wants her help. As a social worker, she's great at helping others, so when she learns more about Nick's reasons for coming home, she can't help but sympathize with him. However, despite her best efforts, she's still bitter about the break-up and to rub it in even more, Nick seems to have only gotten sexier with age. Getting played sucks but ignoring their chemistry sucks more. Only this time, she isn't blinded by his charm. This time, he's playing by her rules.

Prologue

Maybe if I move my arm, she'll wake up! Nicholas gazed upward at the bright sun shining through his oversized skylight, trying to figure out how to get Nurse Thompson out his bed. He could slap himself five times for breaking one of his cardinal rules—sleeping with a co-worker. Nurse Thompson had made several sexual advances on him for the past year, which he had been successful enough to dodge every single one, until last night. She was a beautiful woman; some doctors at the hospital called her downright gorgeous. She was all those things with her smooth, chocolate skin, thick thunder thighs, and a bumble bee ass, molded perfectly for gripping. However, she was a distraction, a substitute for what he'd found but lost.

"Hmmm!"

Nicholas glared down at long, black curls sprawled across his left bicep, and a long, slender arm draped across his chest. His breathing became shallow in anticipation that his unexpected visitor would soon wake up and leave his home. Instead, she snuggled closer under his armpit and inhaled a lung full air, right before he heard a soft snore escape her parted swollen lips. The smeared red lipstick on her right cheek brought back pleasant memories of him devouring her kissable mouth. Nurse Thompson had mastered the art of kissing. Some women were teasers, pretenders, or just didn't have a clue on how to please a man.

But not Nurse Thompson, better known as Erin. She could do wonders with her tongue. She stroked a part of his mouth he didn't even know existed, and the way she sucked on his dick ...

Damn. He shook his head. All he could say was the woman had skills. He almost contemplated keeping her around to ease the tip of loneliness, but he quickly thought better of it. That would be a big mistake. He could never give her what she wanted, or what she deserved.

Reminiscing on the events that led up to his current situation made his stomach turn. He had too much to drink—another reason why he should slap himself—but he was on vacation for the next eight weeks and indulging in an adult beverage was first on his list. Losing his youngest patient yet made him question his abilities for the first time in his career. Amy was ten years old and battling brain cancer. He'd held her tiny, frail hand in her final moments and cursed himself inwardly. *Why couldn't I save her?* That was a hunting question he'd asked himself after every white, cold sheet he'd pulled over his patient's face.

"Get it together Dr. Nick," he voiced out loud.

Little did he know that Erin had trailed him to the

bar down the street of the hospital, after seeing how attached he was to the young patient. One drink turned into two and five and before he knew it, they were back at his place. He was removing her blue scrubs and she had tossed his boxer briefs behind the headboard. It was all a blur now. Him fisting a handful of locs and tugging her head backwards as he plunged in her from behind, and she, riding his dick, like a horse. They did every freaky, nasty thing imaginable and he loved every bit of it.

Now it was time for her to go. Was he wrong for kicking her out, after the night they shared? Maybe! But he didn't care. Something about Erin gave him the notion that she was used to this type of one-night setup. She wasn't a spring chicken, and in his thirty years, he'd been around long enough to know when a woman had a few miles on her.

"Round two, Dr. Brown," she sang in a husky, flirty voice.

Nicholas thoughts stalled, as his eyes darted in Erin's direction, smiling upward at him. "How about round zero?" he replied with a frown.

"Excuse me," Erin uttered as her eyebrows furrowed together.

Nicholas removed the manicured hand laying on his stomach and sat forward on his hunches. "We had a great night together, but it's time for you to go."

Tossing the black comforter back, Erin swung her body out the bed. He wasn't sure if her big doe eyes showed a hint of anger, frustration, or happiness by the way she slid her pink, lacy thong panties up her left leg in a taunting pace.

She placed a hand on her hip and smiled. "See, I

knew you were a natural born asshole. And frankly, that's the type of man I like. I understand, you're not used to people in your space. So, I'll give it time for you to get use to the idea of *us*."

Nicholas frowned. *Did this chick just say us?* There was a reason why he stayed clear of her advancements all this time. He had a mental radar to detect *crazy*, and Erin was that with a capital C. Exhaling a deep breath, he tried to find the words to get crazy out of his house.

"Erin, I didn't mean to lead you on." He briefly paused when he saw a sly smirk spread across her face. *Damn, this bitch is really crazy,* he thought. That fact meant he had to turn off the nice guy act. Because Erin wasn't going to get the fuck out his house, unless he turned into the asshole he was known to be in high school, at the hospital, and to his family and friends. Being that way had never truly gotten him what he wanted, but he had a long list of the shit he'd lost because of his temper.

Hopping out of the right side of the bed, he slid on a pair of denim jeans. Pointing his index finger at Erin, he shouted, "Get the fuck out my house."

Erin cocked her head to the left and reared her body backwards. Her face beamed a bright red, right before he saw a black clog heading toward his direction. He dodged it just in time for the shoe to hit his beige wall.

"Fuck you, Nicholas," she spat. "Fuck you and your sorry ass dick."

One thing Nicholas knew for sure; his dick wasn't sorry. And he decided to remind her of that. "How's it so sorry, when you were screaming about, oh Dr. Nick, your dick is so good. Let me swallow it, put it in my mouth," he taunted. "And for the record, don't be throwing shit in somebody else's home," he warned.

"Screw you," Erin screamed. Sulking, she pulled her shirt over her head and threw her bra in an oversized, blue purse. Scrambling toward the door, she turned around and threw up her middle finger. "And for the record, I got what I wanted."

"Ha!" Picking up two gold hoop earrings from his carpeted floor, he swung open the door and tossed the hoops in her direction. "Don't forget these."

Erin caught them with a quick wave of her hand. "Don't be throwing my shit," she grunted through clenched teeth.

Dismissing her words with a wave of his hand, he said, "Whatever, Erin. And you know what, you're right."

Erin eyebrow raised.

"You did get what you wanted. Some good dick." A slam with the door brought emphasis to his words. When he heard a few curse, words come through the wooden frame door, he smiled and walked over to his refrigerator to down a carton of orange juice.

Shaking his head, he peered out of the kitchen window at his next-door neighbor, Brian, tossing his son in the pool, and his wife, Lauren, laying on a lawn chair smiling and laughing.

He knew if he didn't get his act together, he would run into a wavelength of Erin's. Hoping to become Mrs. Brown. Lately, it seemed that his dream for having a family was fading further into the distance. His shoulders slumped forward, knowing he had chosen a career over a family.

Growing up as an orphan in South Lake Park, known as one of the roughest neighborhoods in Chicago, had prepared him for the world. Sometimes he wondered had it prepared him too much, by never trusting anyone's word or allowing people to stay in his space long enough to hurt him. Another reason he had to show Erin the door. Knowing his own parents didn't want him, sparked the feeling of being unwanted. Yet, five years in therapy sessions couldn't help him to trust or to be open about his feelings. *A total waste of fucking money*, he thought.

The sound of his alarm blaring from his cell phone snapped him from his reverie. Trotting back to his bedroom, he hurriedly swiped the blue screen. Peering down at the phone, he saw he had a miss call. The unexpected caller had his stomach in knots once again. The call had come through at ten o'clock the night before. He had been too intoxicated to hear it and preoccupied by his late-night visitor.

Sitting down on his bed, he stared at the number. He hadn't heard from his foster mother in a few years. He called less after his graduation from medical school. She sent him a few random text messages, which he hardly ever returned.

"Why is she calling now?" he whispered.

Mama Peaches had taken him in off the streets when he was twelve years old. By that time the streets had molded his personality, and being kicked out of every foster home he had ever set foot in, had prompt him to run away from the system and live on park benches, men's shelters, or anywhere he was allowed to lay his head. One night he had found an old mattress that was tossed out on the curb. Snuggling up on the dusty, white mattress he felt a hard grip to his arm. At the fright of being startled, he jumped upward, with his arms up, ready to fight.

Until he recognized the old lady standing before him. She was known around the neighborhood as being feisty and he had heard rumors of her taking in foster kids. However, he wasn't looking for anyone to raise their hand to him again or give him a home just for the government assisted check.

That night changed his life forever; she had offered him into her home, fed him, bathed him, and showed him loved. And when he felt comfortable, she adopted him. Mama Peaches was the reason he was known as one of the top brain surgeons in the world. Not only did she hire him a personal tutor to catch him up with his other peers, but she made sure he exceeded above average.

Laying back on his comforter, he'd wondered all these years, *why did she do it?* She had other foster kids and babysat other kids in the neighborhood … and didn't get nothing out the deal but bad ass kids, tearing her shit up.

He chuckled to himself, remembering the time he almost set her kitchen on fire, trying to cook a pack of hotdogs. The old lady never raised her voice or hand to him. She used lessons to show him the error of his ways —by rewarding him with money when he brought home good grades or took the trash out and taking away video games or time to play outside when he misbehaved.

He had grown to love her, and soon after high school, he was accepted into Florida University, with a full academic scholarship. He'd never looked back at South Lake Park or what he'd left behind. He thought of Mama Peaches over the years, but most importantly, he'd thought of the only woman he's ever loved.

Raina Lawson!

ANGELA'S BOOKS

Distinguished Gentlemen Series:

Invitation to Bid

Secrets, Love & Betrayal Series:

His Betrayal Her Lies

Kept Secrets

Unconventional Love

Once Upon A Bridesmaid series:

Hopelessly Forever

High Class Society Series:

Sealed with a Kiss

Her Sweetest Seduction

Blacksteine Brothers Series:

Love at Center Court

Made in the USA
Las Vegas, NV
01 September 2021